COFFIN COUNTRY

COFFIN COUNTRY

AARON MARC STEIN

PUBLISHED FOR THE CRIME CLUB BY
DOUBLEDAY & COMPANY, INC.
GARDEN CITY, NEW YORK
1976

All of the characters in this book
are fictitious, and any resemblance
to actual persons, living or dead,
is purely coincidental.

First Edition

ISBN: 0-385-11588-1
Library of Congress Catalog Card Number 79–36613
Copyright © 1976 by Aaron Marc Stein
All Rights Reserved
Printed in the United States of America

For
George Gale
Frater, ave atque vale

COFFIN COUNTRY

I

You couldn't ask for a quieter or more peaceful stretch of country. All the same, if you've cocked an ear for a story of peace and quiet, you can forget it.

Let's face it, Charlie. You or I might look to a place like this for getting away from people and for being alone with wind and water, woods and wildflowers, beasts and birds; but there are guys who are not like us. They see any secluded corner only as a theater of operations. Here they can perform the acts that must not be seen. Here they can hide away the things that must not be found, and here, if their deal should go sour on them, they can hide themselves away until, with attention wandering to some other cat's fresher crimes, the heat comes off.

I didn't go up there looking for trouble. That's a thing I don't do. Maybe it's because I'm a peaceful type. More likely it's because I've never wanted for trouble. I don't have to go looking for it. I can be going about my business or going about my pleasure. Trouble always seems to know where I am. It comes and finds me.

Who am I? The name is Erridge, christened Matthew. Mostly people call me Matt and that suits me fine. I've never been a glossy type, I don't shine. My job is engineering, and when the job takes me to one of those quiet and peaceful places, it's got to be because somebody's paying me a fee to advise them on what can be done there toward bringing in the man-made crap that will make it like all other places where metal bangs on metal and progress knocks off peace.

Except that in recent years it's been different. Questions are being asked. Can you do it without air pollution, without water pollution, without discommoding the birds and beasts and fish, without scarring the landscape? If the answer to even one of those questions has to be no, you have a fight on your hands. The locals are up in arms and progress can go stuff itself.

They go to the legislatures. They go to the courts. There have been places where they've gone to their shotguns and their pitchforks. In this particular place, the one I was being paid to look over, the potential for violence might have been stronger than in most places. I knew the history. Just for taking a look I could get me a pitchfork up my ass.

It wasn't virgin territory. The locals around there had been through it before. They were only a couple of years past the finish of their fight and they had only just begun seeing the fruits of their victory. They were not about to let themselves get sucked in again, not for the fast buck, not for the steady buck, not for anything any Greek or Iranian or Wall Streeter could dangle in front of their noses. They'd taken the carrot once, and around those parts carrot allergy had become epidemic.

The old folks could remember how at the beginning it had looked good. When the paper companies first came in, there had been all that money, fat cash payments for the forest lands they were buying up, good construction-crew payrolls all the time the paper mills were building, and, when the mills went into operation, the steady buck, plenty of jobs, and the uninterrupted flow of money on which the local towns could grow and prosper.

Back then it had seemed a good swap—green for green, long green for tall green, money for trees. They'd always had more trees than they thought they needed and never as much money as they would have liked to have. The old ones also could remember how it had begun to go sour. Progress isn't just the one jump forward. You have a small change here and a small change there and nothing hitting hard enough to be noticed when it's happening. Then the changes add up and it comes a time when nobody can kid himself. Nothing is the way it used to be.

First it was the salmon. They weren't coming up the river any more. Then it was the jobs. Guys at drawing boards— smartass types who'd never been within hundreds of miles of the place—designed this gadget and improved that gadget and there would be another machine to do what formerly had been done by many pairs of hands.

The strong boys, who had flocked in off the exhausted farms to take the jobs, didn't like going back to that leaner life they'd run away from. Some of them didn't go back. They hung on in the town and went sour. Those that did go back needed the town for their evenings. There were the bars. There were the girls. There was the front of the drugstore, where a man could stand with his friends even if it wasn't to do any more than to compete at seeing who could spit the farthest.

There had been nothing the locals could do to bring those jobs back, but where they could make a fight they made it. They worked on their state legislators and on their congressmen and their senators. Politicos who didn't come through for them, they punished on election day. The big companies from outside came up with campaign funds, but it was the locals who came up with the votes.

When river dumping of untreated wastes became illegal, the boys back at the drawing boards had to take time out from their work on the labor-saving devices to whip out the antipollution inventions needed for keeping the mills from shutting down. It could be done and it was done. It cost money, but the money was there.

You may have noticed that you're paying more for paper, but the locals noticed that the stuff coming down their river was beginning to look like water again. Better still, the salmon had begun to notice it too. They were coming back home.

Not everything was the way it had been, of course, but as much as they had won back they were going to keep. So when Erridge came waltzing in on them, it had to be a waltz of carefully watched steps. The message on the welcome mat was an unwritten one. It was there, however, and it said: "Get lost."

I wasn't the only unwanted intruder. I was just the one who hadn't declared himself yet. There was Jack Humphrey and Jack had been on the ground before me. The lines had already been drawn up against him, and since everything was concentrated on heading Jack off at the pass, my arrival went all but unnoticed.

That was okay. I could use all the time I could get before I'd have to begin fielding their questions and meeting their arguments. If for a day or two or even a week or two I could pass as nature boy with nothing on my mind but walking in the woods, practicing my rock climbing in the gorge, and watching the salmon fight their way upstream, I would, when my disguise did break down, be in better shape for talking possibilities and making promises. Don't get me wrong, Charlie. I mean promises I could keep.

Jack Humphrey never had a chance because Jack is oil. Not that the people up there aren't like everybody else. They'd like to think cheaper oil. Meanwhile, though, they do think lobsters and clam flats and oyster beds. They have the deep water that can take the supertankers but they also have their fogs and their rockbound coast. Now that they were beginning to have a clean river again, they were anything but ready to start with oil spills in their harbor. Docking facilities? An oil refinery? They weren't even going to listen.

He did keep at it, trying to work on the region's movers and shakers, but all they would ever give him was a deaf ear, and that only because they weren't the types to give him a thick ear. In the violence department he couldn't have been safer. Those very buckos who knew no means of persuasion other than fists, boots, and knives were Jack's allies. They were unwanted allies but they were the only ones he had up there.

In all fairness to Jack that was none of his doing. He never solicited their support and he never incited them. You can call him a catalyst. It took nothing but his appearance on the scene. They were up and roaring. They were the unemployed and, while the rest of the community was smelling oil slicks and air pollution, the Leather Vests were smelling jobs and good pay.

You haven't been up there and you haven't seen them, so you can't be expected to know about the Leather Vests. It's like a uniform. From the waist down they look ordinary enough. The tight blue jeans. The heavy work shoes. The leather belts worn more for menace than for support. Above the belts, though, there's nothing but the leather vests, the vests and the tattoos.

Can you picture a three-piece leather suit? It's been worn so long that the leather is sweat-darkened and it has a greasy shine to it. Discard the jacket and the britches and rip all the buttons off the vest. That's it, Charlie. It's the greasy leather vest hanging open and a generous view of heavily muscled arms, massive chests, and hard, flat bellies. In case you might fail to notice all that display of muscle, your attention had to be drawn to it by the embellishments.

To your way of thinking, skin may just be skin. To these babies it was like blank canvas to a painter or a New York subway car to a graffiti artist. Those guys were a walking folk-museum of tattooing. I never saw a one of them who didn't look like a page of color comics on the hoof.

Mine is not what you'd call a sheltered eye. I've already told you I'm an engineer and that means that no small part of my time is spent with construction crews. I've done jobs in the hot countries where work clothes for the babies who do the heavy stuff runs to sandals at one end, a hard hat at the other, and nothing in between but something like a G-string. I rate myself a connoisseur of tattoos. So if Erridge was impressed, you can take it that those buckos were not merely tattooed. They were lavishly illustrated.

More than that, though, they glowed. It could have been luminous tattooing ink but I haven't heard of any genius inventing that as yet. I think it was just the way they were. No hair on their chests and no hair on their arms, and skin as smooth as any girl's, but there was nothing else in the least girlish about them. Perhaps all that tattooing might kill off body hair. I wouldn't know. Some time I must remember to ask a dermatologist about that. But the way they glowed. Maybe they oiled their bodies or possibly they just sweated grease. That's something else I don't know.

I haven't told you where this is. Go Down East but way down. Follow the coast till you hit the Canadian border. The area I was concerned with straddles the line. The project, if it ever got built, would be on both sides, in Maine and in New Brunswick. It would be in both jurisdictions and subject to the regulations of both. When I talk about the locals, therefore, anything I say goes for both sides of the line.

You hear as much French-Canadian patois on the Maine side as you do in New Brunswick and as much Down East drawl on the New Brunswick side as in Maine. The concerns are the same. The attitudes are the same. It's like a separate country. Whether you come to it from the States or from Canada, if you come from as much as a hundred miles away, you're a foreigner. If they ask any question about you, it is only to assess whether you're a tourist or an enemy. If you do more than pause in passing through, if you show any signs of settling in, you've answered it for them. You're an enemy.

Do you know that stretch of coast? The Bay of Fundy and thereabouts? You wouldn't have to have been up there to have heard about the tides. That's where they run big and powerful. When they come thundering in, they look as though they were about to shove the whole damn Atlantic Ocean up the narrow channels of the rivers. Roaring out, they could be trying to suck the whole of North America dry.

Tourists coming through will pause long enough to catch the next turning of the tide. It's something to see. You can stand at the rim of a gorge and watch white water churn and leap and froth as it cascades down a long stretch of rapids. Only minutes later you're watching it reverse itself to churn and leap and froth while it cascades up the rapids. I'm not kidding. When that tide comes in, it climbs mountains. Wildest thing you ever saw. I guess it's the world's swingingest water.

If you want to know what brought me up that way, that's it, the tides. Since at this stage looking at them was my job, I couldn't make do with the tourist's pause for the one single look. I had to settle in. I needed to watch them day after day in all phases of the moon, in all kinds of weather.

There's power there. Everybody knows that. What the money boys were asking me to tell them was whether we could use it. What could we stick down into that fury of water that would turn us some turbines and make us some electricity. Cheap power, clean power, and power that would never run dry on us. When all the oil and coal and gas have been used up, those monster tides will still be rolling.

You can figure how tempting it had to be for those babies who hold the heavy bread and who want to use it for thinking big. It was tempting because, if it could be made to work, it was going to be great but not because anybody had the notion that it would ever be easy to do.

Stone got stacked up to make the pyramids. Michelangelo got the ceiling painted. The Wright brothers got off the ground. Niagara turns turbines. Nothing's easy, but can it be done? What's more, can it be done without running foul of the house rules? Do it without annoying the salmon, without churning up the clam flats, without disturbing the oysters where they rested in their beds, without lousing up the landscape, without assaulting the local ears with any noise other than the one they'd always lived with, the roar of their wild tidal water. It had to be invisible and inaudible and it had to be geared to provide TLC for all the things that live in the water.

You know about TLC, Charlie? It stands for tender, loving care.

That was the deal. I needed to look at it, study it, and explore it. If possible, I wanted to do all that before I ever tipped my hand. Just promising the locals that ways would be found to do it without hurting anything was never going to be enough. Before they ever heard about it, I needed to be ready to tell them just how it was going to be done.

So I was working at it. I rented a boat and took myself sailing, explored the bay, poked into all its coves. I drove the river road and checked on how far up the river was tidal. I did rock climbs down into the gorge and even chipped off some rock samples. I was trying to act the part of a bird watcher and a fish watcher but I was hoping that, if anyone noticed, I might be allowed a sideline hobby of amateur geology. At ebb tide I shucked out of shoes and socks and went wading in the river. I watched the tide come and go.

I was doing fine. It was lonely, of course, since the locals tended to leave a man alone and they liked it if strangers left them alone. It wasn't unfriendly. Nobody ever passed without saying "mornin'" or "evenin'," but they were so sparing of words that it was only that. Nobody ever expanded it to anything so blabbermouth as "good morning" or "good evening."

I could have had company. Jack Humphrey was there and since it was out of season and we were the only two guests who were using the hotel for anything more than an overnight stop, we did get to know each other. I knew from the first what he was there for. There was too much turmoil about it. Even the passing tourists got wind of it in the course of an overnight stay.

Since I wasn't yet ready to come out in the open, I was no more ready to talk to Jack about what I was doing than I was to tell it to the locals. So for him, since he was the only one who asked, I was a cat on vacation, the complete nature lover making love. He wouldn't have held that against me and I could see that at first sight he had been thinking of me as a possible relief from the Leather Vests, but I saw right off that Erridge had to play it cool. Obviously for Jack Humphrey it couldn't be Erridge or them. If you think of it not as the company he kept but rather as the company that was keeping him, you'll get the picture. They swarmed around him and they wouldn't shake off.

So I had no choice but to do the seclusive bit, maybe even the snob routine. The time was going to come when I would have to get down to cases with the locals and it was an easy guess that getting to be pals with the Vests would start me off with two strikes against me when I would have to go about winning the hearts and minds of the vested interests.

Jack drew his own conclusions. He soon had me pegged for an ecology nut and therefore a potential enemy. To some extent, I suppose, he did have the right of it. I'm not crazy about oil spills, but I'm not so uptight about them that under any ordinary circumstances I would refuse to hoist a couple of friendly ones with a good guy just because he happened to be dependent on an oil company for his bed, board, booze, and benefits.

All the same, I can't say that even if I hadn't been playing the loner that morning, anything would have been different. I had been watching a lot of record tides roar through the gorges of several rivers along that stretch of coast. What I needed to see at that time was something of the other extreme, how much water would be coming through and with how much force at times when the tide would be running at its weakest. I was trying to work up some idea of the parameters we could expect.

Coming into a period of feebler tides, therefore, I couldn't let myself miss out on even one of its turnings. No matter that it meant hauling the reluctant flesh out of the sack at four in the morning for a before-breakfast rock climb, a way-before-breakfast rock climb, Charlie. I had known from the first that the time would come and I had prepared myself a cover for it. I had been toting around an impressive tome on the habits and habitats of nocturnal birds and I had been setting it down in conspicuous places for people to see.

If a guy is nuts about owls, will he not be expected to turn night into day?

When I pulled out of the hotel at four-fifteen that morning, I felt pretty sure there would be nobody up and about to see me go. It wasn't even too likely that there would be anyone up and about to see me return even though it was an early rising community. Just in case, however, I went out with the bird book under my arm. I wasn't going to have to carry it with me when I climbed down into the gorge. I could just leave it on the seat of the Porsche.

Other nights of the week I might have looked for the possibility of running into a late-roaming drunk, but this was a

Sunday night and in a part of the world where Sundays are worse than in Scotland. The Scots won't sell liquor on Sunday except to a traveler, which makes for heavy Sunday traffic. The drinking population of one town drives to the next town and vice versa. Everybody travels.

Sundays where I'm telling you about, though, even the travelers couldn't have any. All the bars shut down and that goes for the hotel bar as well.

It was a black night. Though I didn't have any great distance to drive, much of the driving was half guess and half hope. Fog lay in patches on the land. It was now you see and now you don't. At that time of night I could tell myself that there wouldn't be any traffic to worry about, but when I'd hit a fog patch and I'd see the Porsche's nose disappear in the moment before the damp blindfold wrapped around her windshield, I couldn't tell myself that all the trees that lined the road would have gone home and tucked into bed for the night. They were out there and the road took turns with the river. I had to hope that I'd be taking the same turns.

On a little faith and a lot of care we made it, Baby and I. There was no problem about where I could leave her while I'd be down in the gorge. The road has an observation turnout. The tourists park in it and from there they look down to watch the water when, on the incoming tide, it falls up the rapids. If that was all you wanted, to see water fall up, you could see all you needed from there.

At any tide-turning time during the daylight hours, there would be a line of cars parked up there, but this was owl-and-Erridge time. I found the turnout empty, and I could expect that, but for Baby, it would remain that way, empty of everything but fog and the Porsche.

The fog was a nuisance. I had a good light and it didn't have to be hand carried. I clipped it on to my belt. In the fog I was just as well off without it. It showed me nothing but fog. For the rock climb down into the gorge I had to start out on only feel and memory. I had been up and down those rocks many times in every kind of light and every kind of weather. They didn't worry me. I knew them well enough so that, when I had to, I could do them blind.

Also it wasn't going to be all the way down. The rush of the water through the gorge gives the air a powerful shove. On even the calmest days when there isn't the first breath of breeze stirring anywhere else, the wind down there hits you with gale force. I knew that wind. Every time I had been down there it blew my ears back. No fog can settle in against that kind of wind. Down below, where I would be doing my watching, it would be blown clear.

I left my light switched on even for the upper stretch where it could do me no good. There was going to be that point in the descent where the wind would begin to take hold. Exactly where it would be I had no way of knowing. It could come during one of the trickier passages where I would have no hand to spare from grabbing hold and hanging on. If it did come at a time like that, I would be glad of the light. Even though I was certain that I could do the whole thing blind if I had to, it would only be because I had to. Any time you catch Erridge doing something the hard way, you've got to know it won't be from choice.

I climbed over the guardrail. The fog-smeared metal was slick under my hands. The rocks were going to be wet and slick as well, but I had been expecting that. For at least the lower half of the climb they were always wet and slick. The spray kicked up off the rapids reaches high and, even when the walls of the gorge are sunbaked during the slack of the tide, that never lasts long enough to bake all the water off them. The mossy spots ooze water any time you touch them. Under a hot sun they might ooze tepid water. That was the outside limit of difference.

I had, of course, expected that by the time I was down

into that level of perpetual soak, I would also be down to the level of the high wind, clear of the fog, and able to see my way for negotiating the slippery stuff. Obviously that was not to be. This was a night when Matthew was getting none of the breaks.

By holding my wrist close to the light on my belt I could read my watch dial. Having started out as early as I did, I should have had some time to waste. Fifteen minutes or, at worst, ten before I would have to start down. My watch said different. I knew that I'd done the drive from the hotel at nothing like normal Porsche pace. I knew that the fog had slowed me down, but I hadn't realized by how much. We had come along, Baby and I, at what couldn't have been much better than a caterpillar creep.

So I was left with only a five-minute margin. To hang on up at the rim for five minutes in the hope that in such time something would lift to give me better visibility was hopeless. I'm no fog expert, but it had always seemed to me that fogs took longer for the process of lifting off than they do for settling in.

Also my five-minutes to spare was something of an illusion. My watch was telling me what had happened to the margin I'd allowed myself on driving time. If the Porsche-born Erridge could have been slowed down that much, how much speed could I expect to get out of an Erridge on the hoof?

Doing it blind would have to mean doing it slowly. I might not need all of the extra five minutes for getting myself down there but at best I was going to need a sizable chunk of it.

Edging along with one hand on the rail, I kept the other one free for groping through the fog ahead of me, feeling for my first landmark. That one would be easy. It was a blackberry bush that grew along the railing. You don't have to see

a blackberry bush to recognize it. As soon as your hand
comes down on the thorns, you know you're there.

My hand came down on it and good. I got it in the ball of
my thumb and it wasn't just getting pricked. That thumb
got stabbed. It was no great disaster. It wasn't going to crip-
ple me, but it was one helluva lot more than I had bar-
gained for.

You know blackberry bushes, Charlie. Who doesn't?
They're tough and they're mean. Give one a brush and you'll
come away criss-crossed with bloody scratches. Have you
ever hit one, though, that worked more than the surface of
you? This one was an old acquaintance and it had always
been like all other blackberry bushes. So this one night it
goes savage, sending a thorn driving into me as though it
had ideas of impaling me at the rim of that gorge and hanging me up there to dry.

I pulled back and sucked at the thumb. Blood before
breakfast? Nobody's favorite eye-opener. All the same, I had
located the blackberry bush. I had my bearing or I thought
I had. I started forward confidently enough and immediately ran into an obstacle, something that should never have
been there. It explained the peculiar behavior of the blackberry bush, but it didn't explain itself. It made no sense.

Any time you hit one of those thorny bushes you have to
expect that the thorns will get you, but they don't grow out
of anything rigid. The bush is pliable. It yields to pressure.
For a thorn to drive in the whole of its length it has to be
growing out of something far less movable. What I had now
run into was just that, something far less movable. My knee
hit it. When I reached down to explore it, my hand first
touched leather and then cold, wet metal. Bellied up against
it with my light, I couldn't see the whole of it, just a small
area with the rest of it hidden in the fog.

It was a motorcycle. It was parked on a rock ledge where
the blackberry tangle would conceal it from the road turn-

out. Dig what had happened, Charlie? When my thumb hit that thorn, the thorn had no place to go but all the way in. Backed by the motorcycle it had been held rigidly in position. Before it could have been moved back under pressure, the pressure would need to have been heavy enough to topple the motorcycle.

If that was one small mystery cleared up, it was another small mystery presented. Why should anyone who had a motorcycle to park be so dead set on not leaving it parked in the obvious place, leaning against the guardrail up on the road turnout? If the guy was afraid it might be stolen, with a chain and a padlock it would have been no trick to anchor it to the guardrail. It would certainly have been a lot safer up there than where it was out on the rock ledge where anybody making the climb down into the gorge might come up against it hard and send it toppling to bounce down from rock to rock and drown its wreckage in the rapids at the bottom.

Safety, furthermore, was only a part of it. There was also the muscle and the sweat. Lifting the motorcycle over the guardrail had taken a lot of lifting. Sneaking it along the ledge to its place of concealment behind the blackberry thicket had taken a lot of ticklish maneuvering.

I worked my way around the motorcycle and started the climb down over the rocks. I had to give most of my mind to remembering the footing and the available handholds and locating them by feel and by memory in the fog and the dark. Although I can't say I put the motorcycle mystery out of my mind, I was too busy with the moment-to-moment necessities of the climb to put any full head of steam into my thinking about motorcycles.

Even without heavy thinking, though, there were some assumptions that did jump out at me. It could be that Erridge wouldn't be alone in his climb down into the gorge. Maybe this time someone had gone down ahead of me.

Someone who was operating as I was, studying the terrain while he preferred to have his purposes go unknown?

It seemed possible, but only possible. Hardly inevitable. That he had gone to all that work and trouble to hide his motorcycle off the road because he was exploring and he didn't want anyone knowing what he was doing seemed a good enough bet. It didn't have to mean that he was doing this exploring in what I had come to think of as Erridge's territory. It was more likely that he was somewhere up topside stealing chickens. One thing was for sure. Down in the gorge there was nothing anybody would want to swipe. Rock fragments? Specimens of moss? A hatful of spray? Those were all there for the taking, but who'd want them and who, apart from Matthew Erridge, would have any reason for being so secret about it?

I thought some about my bird-watching cover and had to recognize that, put to the test, it wasn't going to cover much. If I ran into company while I was inching my way down those rocks, I'd have to be something else. It would have to be something moderately foolish, but who's to say Erridge can't be a fool? For this night, perhaps, he was going to have to be a mountain-climbing nut out to get some practice under his belt against the possibility that sometime night would catch up with him when he was part way up the Matterhorn.

If I was going to meet someone down there, it seemed likely that it would be a bucko who would be in no position for asking questions, but that wouldn't make much difference. He'd have questions about me in his mind just as I was having questions about him in mine. I was getting ready to answer unasked questions. I didn't want him to go off speculating about me and maybe spreading his speculations out among the locals.

Insofar as I was thinking at all, I was beginning to think that meeting this baby could be fun. Maybe he would be practicing rock climbing as well and we could swap alpinist lies we'd be making up as we went along. With a feeling that was almost regret I told myself that any meeting would be most unlikely. If Erridge had been stealthy about his coming here tonight, Mr. Whoeverhewas had been that much stealthier. I had left the Porsche up on the road turnout. I hadn't taken her up in my brawny arms and hoisted her over the guardrail to tuck her out of sight in any blackberry thicket.

I was wearing my light. Even though it was no great help to me for seeing anything in the fog, it did cast its glow. Anybody down in the dark, though he might not see me coming, would see something of my light. All he would have to do, if he wanted to avoid me, would be to stop on one of the ledges and edge along it well out of the way of any feasible path of descent. I could think of four or five places where it could be done. If there was someone else doing this under these nothing conditions of visibility, he would have to be someone who knew the places at least as well as I did.

So he was such a someone and he did know them. I was halfway down. Although still blanketed in the fog, I had begun to notice some changes. They were encouraging changes. They had to mean that only a body length or a little more than that farther down I would be coming out under the fog and into the clearer air of the lower gorge where my light would illuminate for me what I'd come to watch.

The taste of the fog was changing. It had begun to be noticeably salt on my lips. When I ran my tongue over them, I got a distinct taste of it. It wasn't the taste of sweat. That's salty too, but it isn't the salt of spray. There was a second change as well, and that was a verification of the first. The touch of the fog against my skin was beginning to have a chill on it that it hadn't had up above.

I was on one of the ledges and I was betting that when I

would clamber down to the next ledge I would feel the wind there and begin to see the fog swirl under the push of it. I crouched at the edge and ran my hand over the rock face below, feeling for the irregularities that were to be my footholds for working myself down.

I didn't find them. My fingers touched something that was neither rock nor moss. It was longer than moss and softer. Don't ask me whether I knew right off it was hair or reasoned out later that it had to be. Things happened too fast and too much all at once for any chance of separating out any individual pieces of it.

I'm telling it as I remember it or think I remember it. You're feeling for things in the dark and you touch something that is totally unexpected. There's the quick reflex that wants to jerk your hand back but with it there's the curiosity, or more than a curiosity, it's a need to know, that pushes your fingers to explore it further.

I just don't know whether I was jerking my hand back or moving it in for further exploration. Whichever I was doing, however, was immediately knocked off. A tight grip slammed down on my extended forearm and a quick downward jerk hauled me out of my crouch at the rim of the ledge. I came down like the little cherubim in some old painting, ass end up.

Any reasonable expectation would say that landing head first on the ledge below I must have cracked my head against the rock and that such a crack would knock me silly. Ever been hit for the count, Charlie? If it's never happened to you, then you can just take my word for it. I know. You never know what hit you. Maybe there'll be someone around who can tell you afterward or maybe you can figure it out for yourself later by taking an inventory of contusions and abrasions. Anything like that, however, comes later. When it's happening to you, you know from nothing.

II

Now it's that later we were just talking about. Getting knocked out ordinarily will not mean that you are going to stay out for any great length of time. Prolonged unconsciousness from a knockout blow occurs only if it's a blow that's done you some major damage, like leaving you concussed or with a fractured skull. I'm talking, of course, about how it's going to be if you take the knockout blow at a time when you are in average good health. Sick people maybe would take a longer time to come surging up out of it. I don't know. Ailing has never been one of my things.

Maybe it was the icy splash of the water that brought me to but it's likely that I'd just had my time under and would have been coming up out of it even without the water. The cold shock of it, however, did at least wash out for me any halfway stages there might have been. There was no period of lying around while I gathered up my wits. The cold water did that much for me. It gathered them up, clear and sharp, and it slapped me with them.

And, brother, did I need them? You know how fog-blinded I had been before I was jerked off that ledge and sent tumbling ass over teakettle. Now it was worse. Now I couldn't see at all. The light was still on my belt. I felt for it with my hand and it was there and it seemed to be intact, certainly not shattered. I could feel it but I couldn't see it. I couldn't see anything, not even fog.

I told you that I had been coming far enough down the rock face for the fog to have begun taking on something of the taste of the salt spray. Now the taste was up to full strength, but there was a smell along with it. It was the smell of dead fish, of fish that had been too long dead and too long off the ice on a hot day. Let us not mince words, Charlie. That was no smell. It was an overwhelming, gut-blasting stink.

It was there and it hung around me as though it was anchored to me, which made not the first bit of sense. The wind was roaring past me. I was hearing it and from the waist down I was feeling it. It was coming cold up the legs of my britches and it was whipping the cuffs of them around my ankles. A wind that felt as though it wouldn't need much more force to blow all of Erridge's 190 pounds away should have been more than enough to be blowing anything as weightless as a fish stink out of Errige's nose range.

I was moving my hands, but quickly it came to me that I wasn't moving them much. I could run them along my belt and feel of my lamp but I couldn't move them out away from my body. I couldn't understand that right off. I had to think about it some, but I had no time for thinking. A second icy splash of water told me that much. There was more of it than there had been in the first splash and this second time there was noticeably more oomph behind the way it hit me.

I sat up. Leaving any thinking I might do for later, I scrambled to my feet. Doing it no hands on a slick and uneven rock ledge had its hazards. If I gave any thought to the very good chance that I might lose my footing, it was only to tell myself there was no help for it. I'd end up no worse off than I would be if I just stayed where I was. The only hope was to get myself up and out of there. Any other way I was dead.

I knew where I was. I knew the place and the time. I was on the lowest of the ledges on the rock face of the gorge. If I fell off that one, I'd be in the rapids and down to only two possibilities, both final. Either I would die by drowning or I'd be battered to death when the water bounced me from rock to rock.

Staying put on that ledge was hardly a better choice. The tide had begun its turn. The first splash of icy water had come with the turning. The greater weight and force of the second splash measured for me the building of the mass of water. It had begun doing that great trick the tourists come to watch. It was falling uphill and this time it was falling on me.

I knew the way it came. I had been studying it long enough. It was no slow rise. It didn't come creeping up. When it hit the river mouth, it was confined and compressed by the walls of the gorge. It came tumbling up the rapids as a wall of wildly turbulent water. If I stayed where I was, it was going to come pouring down on me to sweep me off the ledge and into the rapids.

I had to climb up out of there and climbing no hands was impossible. My arms were tied down to my sides but not tightly. I could move them any way I liked so long as it was movement that kept them close to my body. The constriction took me at about the middle of my forearms.

That did seem a peculiar place for tying a man. You'd expect it would be at the wrists. Peculiar it was, but I was accepting it and gratefully. Tied at the wrists I would have had no chance. This way it seemed to me that I might have possibilities. I pushed out hard with my arms just on the chance I could break it. That was no good. It felt as though it might have given a little, but it didn't break.

I tried the next best thing. That was pushing down with my elbows. I felt the thing that was binding me slide up my forearms about an inch. I tried a second downward push with my elbows and I gained another inch, but that was even a bigger gain. I now had it up far enough so that I could bend my arms a little, and with that it slid up higher and freed the whole of my forearms.

It wasn't perfect. I couldn't get my shoulders into anything I tried to do and I had only forearm reach, but I could feel the water swirl over my shoetops. It was sucking at my feet. It was make do with as much as I had and hope it would be enough to get those feet up out of there and with no further delay.

The distance between the lowest ledge and the one next above it I remembered as being a relatively short one. It was seven to eight feet at the most but that was going to be all I would need. On this night of minimal tide it would be the difference between total immersion and merely being drenched with spray.

I scrambled at it and made it just enough to bring my feet up out of the water. Then I went for a handhold that was just out of reach. Stretching for it with that limited forearm stretch of mine, I pulled myself too far off balance and nothing held. I crashed down and landed flat on that lowest ledge with the water pouring over me.

I felt the push of it and I had no delusion that I could do myself any good fighting it. There was no way Erridge could go except the way that water was going to carry him. Remember King Canute? He couldn't bring it off and it wasn't for the lack of any great modern knowhow. There just isn't any how, Charlie. A roaring tide is a roaring tide. Battle it and you're hopelessly out of your class.

This time, with my forearms free, I had some help from my hands when I fought my way to my feet. That, however, didn't put me in a better position. It was a lot worse. Flat down on the ledge I'd had more stability than I could have up on my feet. I was standing on slick rock with the water battering my ankles as it quickly built the force that was going to knock my feet out from under me.

I did the only thing I could do. Grabbing a good hold on the rock face, I crouched down to bring myself low enough for the water to slap against my thighs. I held it that way, feeling the water rise and feeling the force of it build up. It was coming in crashing waves now and I was keeping a count on its timing, measuring off for myself on each surge of it the interval between the first hint of upward movement and the moment of its crashing crest.

Letting go wasn't easy. Every instinct was fighting to keep my hands clamped down hard on the holds they had found in the rock face. I remember that I talked to them.

"Okay, hands," I told them. "Like it or not, you've got to co-operate. Hang loose, hands, and be ready to grab and hang on. I'm promising you. There will be something to grab."

Inside my head I knew there was no certainty. I was telling myself that there had better be something to grab, but it seemed better to keep my hands in ignorance of my doubts.

The surge began building. As the force of it came up at me, I shot myself up out of my crouch and let the water take my feet out from under me. I went with it, co-ordinating my spring with the lift of the water. It was like scaling a high fence with a buddy under you to give you a powerful boost. It wasn't too like that, of course, because no friend is going to be that rough and no buddy ever had mitts that were as cold as that water.

Right on cue my hands did what they were told to do. They let go and as far as they could reach, they reached. My right caught the ledge and grabbed. I got my left up beside it and it scrambled for a hold. For the moment that was good enough. I hung there while I walked the rock face with my toes, working myself up as high as I could. A couple of surges ran by under me while I was doing it but they weren't reaching high enough to pull at me. They were just slapping me on the ass as they went by.

I waited. I knew that the big water was coming and it wasn't going to be a long wait. If I could have had the full use of my arms, I wouldn't have needed to wait for it. I could have pulled myself high enough to have scrambled on to that next ledge, the one from which I was now hanging by my finger tips. Not able to get any upper arm or shoulder action into it, I couldn't do it on my own. I had to wait for my icy-fingered friend to give me the big boost from below.

Surge after surge came by and I kept myself hanging loose, riding each successive crest and keeping a measure in my mind of how much higher it lifted me each time through. If I could have waited for the top of the tide, it would have been easy. I knew how high it would be reaching, just high enough to lap the ledge I was hanging from. If I could wait that long, riding each successive crest and hanging on, it would lift me right up on to the ledge I was scrambling for.

Waiting, however, was one thing I knew I couldn't allow myself. My hands were holding but I was coming to the place where I could know it only from the fact that I was still hanging there and not being grabbed by the water to be dashed down into the rapids. Both hands had gone numb and the numbness was spreading through my arms. It would be a matter of minutes, perhaps even of no more than seconds, before I would lose control. When that happened the rush of water was going to tear me loose from the rock face and I'd be finished.

I couldn't wait for the water to boost me to safety. I had to do some of it for myself and I had to gamble on my judging it right, picking the crest that would give me just enough to let me make it the rest of the way by my own scrambling.

It came and I scrambled. I had waited, though, till just before my hands and arms would have gone totally nerveless. As it was, they were getting their messages through so poorly that I knew I had it made only through feeling the scrape of the ledge rim against my chest and belly.

I hung there. My chin and my elbows found dents in the rock and they pressed hard into them, helping me anchor myself. I rested with that, waiting for my breath to come back. I was past thinking that it was the fish-stink breath. It didn't matter how it smelled. I needed it.

Maybe good air would have done it for me faster, but this sufficed. My breathing began to slow. My heart beat started taming down. Sensation crept back into my hands and arms. All the way up to my knees I was taking a buffeting from the water and with each crest it was reaching higher, but it wasn't getting enough grab on me to haul me down. I could wait till just short of the time when it would rise high enough to again give me a battle, but then I wondered if I would know when it was just short of that time. I could misjudge it and wait till it was strong enough to take me.

Did I decide against waiting or did that thought send me into one of those panic scrambles that cuts loose from any decision-making process? I don't know. It seems to me that I was clawing and scrambling, pulling my legs up and getting all of me up on to the safe ledge before I ever knew what I was doing.

A man can do that, scare himself into action when good sense would hold him back. Whatever way it was, fear showed good enough judgment. Between us, fear and me, we made it. I got my legs up and I could lie and pant and pull myself together without any worry about the water getting at me to any extent that could matter.

It was drenching me with freezing spray and, if I lay there long enough, it would lap up around me to soak me afresh, but that would be the worst it could do. I was above the level where it could reach me with its violence. As I pulled myself together, I also began taking stock of myself.

It was no rope or strap that was constricting my arms. It

was a burlap sack. It had been pulled down over my head and its drawstring closing had been pulled tight to bind my arms to my sides. Now that I no longer had to use my hands for hanging on, I found that I could wriggle and shrug and push and in that way work my way out of it. It made all the difference. I could see again and since, as I had expected, I was now down below the fog and my light was still working, visibility within limits was excellent. At my level and looking down to where the water just below me was rampaging up the rapids all was clear, the churning surge of the tide, the glitter of the spray, the gleaming surfaces of the wet rock. Looking up, I could see nothing. The fog hung no more than what appeared to be a few feet above my head. I could almost reach up and lose my hand in it.

Breathing was also a lot better once I had the sack off my head. I wasn't clear of the stench of dead fish. My skin and my clothes were smelling of it and I still had the sack dangling from my hand. It was so strong that I was going to have to put a lot more distance between it and my nose before I could be clear of the stink of it. With it all, nevertheless, I did have the good feel of breathing air again, air instead of vaporized rotten fish gut.

I had a large assortment of aches and pains and even though they were dulled down by the numbing effect of the cold water, I wasn't unaware of them. I sat up and began taking stock of injuries. Feeling of myself, I located large areas of bruise on a shoulder and a hip and assorted other such areas almost everywhere else. I ran my hands over my head, feeling for lumps and prodding for sore spots. I found none of either but at the back of my neck just below the base of my skull I located a spot that had been to the wars. It read like a book. Erridge hadn't fallen into a sack and tumbled down to land on his head and knock himself out.

It had been the quick chop to the back of his neck if it hadn't been a rabbit punch. Once that had taken him out, the sack had been hauled down over his head and the drawstring had been pulled tight to bind his arms to his sides. Neatly packaged that way, old Matthew had needed no more than a nudge to tumble him off that fog-shrouded ledge up above so that he would drop down into the gorge.

Obviously it had been expected that it wouldn't matter much whether the tumble would take him all the way down the rocks or whether it would land him on that lowermost ledge where the rising tide would come roaring in only a little later to dispose of him with even greater efficiency.

It was possible that it wouldn't have mattered too much even if my fall had ended at this higher level, on this ledge where I was now sitting. Even that would have been sufficient for having me out of the way for a while. There was no certainty that the intention had been to finish me off. All that was certain was that somebody had wanted me out of the way and had not felt the least concern about the possibility that he might have been murdering me in the process.

I got up on my feet and looked at the fish sack. I had had more than enough of the smell of it. I could be a lot more comfortable if I tossed it into the water and rid myself of it. I began balling it up in my hands to put it into shape for giving it a good heave. I didn't want it just drifting down to snag on a rock where it might hang out of reach of my hands but not out of reach of my nose.

I was cocking my arm to pitch the sack when this other thing came hurtling past me. It didn't miss me by much, but it did miss me. If it hadn't, it would most certainly have done the job that the rabbit punch and the sack and the tide had missed out on doing. My light caught it as it bounced on the ledge but it was only for its moment of bounce. It rolled and went on down to disappear in the churning water.

It went by so fast that it was already gone by the time I registered on what it was. Do I have to tell you? It was that motorcycle I had come on in its hiding place behind the blackberry thicket. I couldn't believe that any accident had dislodged it from its parking place. I did have the thought that I might have been seen in my scramble for safety and that the motorcycle had then been the projectile readiest to hand. Had the intention been to drop it on Erridge and with it knock him into the rapids or had there been no idea more elaborate than just dropping the thing?

I looked up. The fog was still there, a solid layer of it over my head. I did have the light and I'd made no move to shield it, but the fog had been and still was shield enough. Nobody up above would be seeing even the faintest glimmer of the light.

I still had my arm cocked for throwing the sack, but now I was thinking better of it. Now it seemed to me that there might be something copycat about doing it. My unknown adversary seemed to be bent on getting rid of things: Erridge, the sack, the motorcycle. For me to throw the sack away, wouldn't that be playing into his hands if it wasn't aiding and abetting?

The thought gave me pause and then there was something more. Holding the sack balled up in my hand, I was feeling something. It was something small. Through the sacking it felt round and hard like a pebble or a nut or an acorn. I couldn't think of anything else it might be without going far out.

A diamond? A diamond that size seemed most unlikely. After all, this was nowhere near Elizabeth Taylor country. In any case, I was curious. I let the bag drop loose, plunged my arm down into it, and fished around. My fingers closed on the thing. As I'd expected, it was no diamond. It wasn't even a pebble. Even though pebbles are softer than diamonds, that's only something you've learned. They aren't noticeably softer to the touch. Though this thing wasn't soft, it did yield slightly when pinched between my finger and my thumb. Its surface wasn't smooth. It was ridged except for one spot that had a soft and fuzzy feel to it.

I pulled it out of the sack and held it in the full beam of my light. It was a button, but no ordinary button. It was a leather button, made of narrow thongs tightly woven over a wooden or metal core. Spherical in shape, it rolled in the palm of my hand and its soft, fuzzy spot turned up. When the button had torn away, it had taken with it a bit of the fabric to which it had been sewn.

The fuzz was pale, the color of butter or maybe of the runny inside of a perfectly ripened Brie cheese. The fuzz was also soft, softer than anything a sheep could grow and softer than any synthetic. If it wasn't vicuña, it would have to be cashmere.

I have a jacket with buttons very much like it, but this was no button of mine. The leather of mine is darker and the jacket is a gray tweed, rugged and rough to the touch. Anyhow I wasn't wearing the jacket that night. It was hanging in the closet back at the hotel.

I stowed the button away in the pocket of my shirt. It was a pocket with a fasten-down flap. Stowed there, it couldn't possibly roll out and lose itself. I still had ahead of me the climb back up to the road and no guarantee on what I might be meeting on my way up to the Porsche.

Thinking of Baby got me moving. I didn't think anyone could heave the Porsche up over the guardrail and tumble her down into the gorge, but there was a bucko about who might well have had a thing against luxuries. He had done violence to a coat that could only have been a product of Savile Row bespoke tailoring. Could I rely on him to be gentle with my Porsche?

I tucked the sack into my belt in back, letting it hang down behind me. You know, the way a football center wears the towel for the quarterback to dry his hands on. I had decided not to get rid of it. If now some more of its stink rubbed off on me, it couldn't matter much. If you are going to be spectacularly malodorous, and I was that already, a little more or a little less could be of no consequence.

I switched off the light. I was climbing up into the fog where it couldn't be the least bit of good to me. If there was anybody still up there, it might give him some slight foreknowledge of my approach. That wasn't any enormous if either. He had been up there only moments before to shove the motorcycle off the ledge at the top.

I started the climb. I was certain that the fog had me covered. Nobody up there could possibly see me coming. I was moving as quietly as I could and I would be okay there. The water down below was at full rampage. There was no sound I could make that would be heard over that thunder.

I was left with only one possibility. If there was anyone up there, he would almost certainly smell me coming, but there was no help for that. Dumping the sack could make little difference. It had long since perfumed my hair and my skin and my clothes.

I hauled myself up ledge to ledge, climbing into the fog. If anything, it now seemed thicker than it had been when I had been climbing down through it. It was, however, changing color. What had been a black blanket was now more the color of one of those dark gray army blankets. Somewhere above the fog dawn would be pulling up over the horizon by its rosy fingers.

That's pretty, isn't it? In case you haven't noticed, it isn't Erridge. It's Homer more or less. If any of those good people who in years gone by did the Herculean job of sweating some book learning into Matthew Erridge are reading this, they can see that it wasn't all in vain. Bits of it did stick, and from time to time it does me a lot of good.

Like this time I'm telling you about. Thinking about rosy-fingered dawn as I was climbing up through the fog was far more relaxing than thinking about what I might find waiting for me at the top of the climb.

I made it all the way and I met nothing. Skirting the blackberry thicket was easy because now there was no motorcycle to be skirted as well. The fog still lay on the road but it had turned gray and pearly. Dawn had come but it was still that time of soft light between the dawn and the sunrise. There wasn't the first hint of the muffled glare fog will take on when you have sun behind it and it's trying to burn its way through.

In the mist I could make out the familiar shape. The Porsche was standing in the turnout where I'd left her. It remained to be seen whether Baby had been molested.

I vaulted the railing and walked slowly around her. I kicked her tires and gave her a superficial inspection. She looked fine, nothing to suggest that anyone had touched her. I did for a moment consider the possibility of dynamite or gelignite wired to her ignition, but checking for that can be tricky. Too many people have learned about that possibility.

Your subtle bomber finds a way to get his licks in earlier. You raise the hood to check for any of those extra little packages that might have been wired there and that will be the trigger. She blows as the hood comes up.

Thinking about it, I relaxed. It just wasn't in the picture. Taking the most cheerful view of what hit me, the purpose had been to put Erridge out of action during a period when it would have been inconvenient to have him around. It wasn't easy holding onto this most cheerful view since the methods used could have been called disproportionately drastic.

Safety, therefore, called for taking the gloomiest view. The purpose had been to put Erridge out of action permanently. I couldn't imagine why. I had made no enemies in the vicinity, but facts are facts. I'd been knocked cold, tied up in the sack, and booted down into the gorge; and all of this just at the time when the tide was about to come rampaging in.

It seemed evident that this procedure had been followed in full confidence that it would take care of the permanent elimination of one Matthew Erridge. It would have taken little time and not much trouble to pick up a rock and beat his brains in with it. The dead body, booted down into the gorge, would then have certainly been taken by the water and given so much further battering against the rocks in the rapids that, even if the body had ever been recovered, no post-mortem examination could have determined that death had come by anything but accident.

You may be thinking that pains had been taken to produce a corpse that, when recovered, would be yelling foul play. By what kind of an accident could a man put his head in a sack and tie his arms down to his sides with the sack drawstring? It's a good thought but only because you don't know those rapids and you don't know that water.

Between water and rocks it would take only moments before a man down in there would have been stripped naked and not much more than moments before the pounding of water and rocks would have him down to the bone and breaking up. I hadn't seen it, but I knew without seeing how the rapids must have taken the motorcycle, dismantling it, churning its broken bits around till even the bits would be abraded beyond any recognition of what they once had been.

As flesh goes, the Erridge flesh is average tough but it's one helluva way short of being steel. So to the mind of the adversary it must have seemed that Erridge had been eliminated. Further action toward making sure of his demise would have been waste motion and it would also have given the show away.

The Porsche stands there in the turnout. It goes on standing there unclaimed for longer than can seem reasonable and Erridge has disappeared. He has vanished but he's left all his stuff in the hotel room and his hotel bill stands unpaid. Okay. His mangled remains are fished out of the rapids. Is Baby going to be left standing there up against the guardrail to wait for him when it's obvious that he'll never be driving her again? Of course, not. The fuzz would drive her out of there and put her in safe keeping against the time when the executors of Matt's estate would be laying claim to her.

But she doesn't drive out of there. She's been wired for extinction and she blows up. Doesn't any hope of an accident theory blow up with her? Of course, it does. Nothing to gain, Mr. Adversary, and everything to lose. But wait a tick. Suppose Erridge is shot with luck. Suppose he does land on that ledge short of the rapids. Suppose he does come to before the water comes up high enough to take him. Suppose he gets up enough strength to snap the drawstring of the fish sack. It's only a string. It's no great rope or steel chain. It wasn't made for trussing Erridge up. It was made only for holding the mouth of the sack tied so that nothing out of a catch of crabs or lobsters or fish could escape from it.

Suppose all those supposes and you have Erridge climbing up out of the gorge alive-alive-o and bringing up with him the sack and the button for the fuzz to use in tracing their owner. It's not likely to happen but if it does, nobody's going to be thinking accident then. Erridge will be around to testify and Erridge will know better, not to speak of the sack and the button. They will be evidence. Just for insurance then, to set at ease the mind of some cat who wears both belt and suspenders a well-timed explosion could put Erridge out of testifying range and at the same time eliminate the sack and the button.

Now that was a thought. It was a potent thought since it brought with it pictures of some of the locals I'd been seeing. There were buckos about who did wear both belt and suspenders. I'd seen them and some of them were Leather Vests.

Potent, but not persuasive. If there had been any thought that the sack could have been traced, it would never have been used. My arms could have been bound to my sides without it. My own belt could have been used for that and it would have worked a lot better than the sack drawstring. So that left the button. That button with the telltale fuzz of fabric still sewn tight to it could be traced. There couldn't be many like it in that part of the world. The few that were would be sewn on a coat which in that locality would be widely recognized.

An even more potent thought, but one that was even less persuasive. It was crazy to believe that my ill wisher could have had the faintest notion that the button had come off and that it had landed in the sack. The button was my secret. He would never dream that I could have it.

So logic was telling me that the Porsche had to be all right. Nobody had converted Baby into a bomb. I unlocked her trunk and tossed the fish sack into it, taking just a moment for inspection as I did it. It was the way I'd been figuring it. Trying to move my arms away from my body, I had put enough stress on the drawstring to snap it. That had been how the mouth of the sack had come loose enough for me to work it up my forearms. From that time till I'd struggled all the way out of it, I'd had nothing holding me but the sack itself.

I shut the trunk and climbed aboard. For some moments I did hesitate before I touched the ignition, but I ran through the logic of it again, and logic took hold. I let Baby have it and she came up with her usual sweet purr. We pulled away from the guardrail and she set her nose to the road back to town.

I don't know what she had in mind, but I was about to

have her take me straight off to the police station. Honest Injun. Cross my heart. All that jazz.

What else was there for a cat to do? Okay, he has nine lives, but hadn't he just fresh used one of the nine up? Oughtn't he go just a little stingy with spending the other eight, if there were still eight to go? In other places and at other times there had been other close calls. I wasn't about to go digging them out of memory and adding them up to see whether I did still have any of the eight spares left to me.

And that wasn't the whole of it. There was also the law-abiding-citizen jazz. Wasn't it the duty of a good citizen to take his story to the fuzz and put the evidence into their hands? Why should a prominent part of that evidence be offending only my nose and Baby's? Surely the constituted authorities should not be deprived of their sniff at it. They're the bloodhounds, aren't they?

So Matthew Erridge is on his way to the police station to tell his story. Obviously any lawbreaker confronted with a compulsion to blab to the fuzz will, en route to the station house, be rehearsing in his mind the story he is going to tell. As I tooled along making cautious progress through the recurrent fog patches that still hung on the road—the sun was going to have to be well up before those would begin to burn off—I found that what goes for the lawbreaker can go for the law-abiding cit as well.

You tell people, and these were going to be official sort of people, that you were all wrapped up in fog and the sound of rushing waters when out of nowhere you got chopped, knocked unconscious, tied up in a fish bag, and tossed down into the gorge. Because you are a lucky bloke and Superman to boot, you explain to them that you did a Houdini and extricated yourself from mortal peril, but that there was a motorcycle and, since it wasn't as smart as Erridge, it did go down to destruction in the rapids.

You further tell them that you discovered that you weren't alone in the fish bag. Along with you and its stink, the latter of which speaks for itself, the sack contained this Savile Row-type button which, you can see, still has attached to it a tiny scrap of somebody's super-luxurious coat.

Think you're going to get away with telling them that and no more? Have another think, Erridge. Take yourself a lot of thinks and you'd better make them good. There will be questions and not one answer you can clam up on.

Where were you when this attack occurred?

What were you doing there in the dark and the fog?

Can you think of anything that might explain this attack that was made on you?

Who are you?

Where did you come from?

What is your purpose in hanging around these parts?

Do you dig my dilemma, Charlie? It was much too soon for me to answer those questions, but they would have to be answered. Also the answers could play no games with the truth. I'd been going along under my bird-watcher and nature-lover cover. I had been planning to blow my cover when I would be ready to blow it and I had known from the first that when such time came there would probably be those who would look with extra suspicion on anything I would have to say to them because they would feel that for all this time I had been acting out a lie.

With some people it was going to be that way, but there was no help for it. I'd been hoping I would be able to win even those people over to the thought that I hadn't deceived them. I had been acting right out in the open and they had misinterpreted my actions. This far, however, I had spoken no lies. I hadn't told anyone what I was up to, but nobody had asked me.

At the police station the questions would be asked. Do I say I was out looking for owls I could watch? Down in the gorge? Nobody was going to believe that and later, when it would come time to talk tide-harnessing and electric power, I would have blown any hope for credit. I would be asking them to have faith in my promises. Who puts his faith in a sneak and a liar? I was going to be but dead.

I drove by the police station without even looking at it. I drove back to the hotel and told nothing to anybody.

III

It was still early. The hotel wasn't awake yet. I ran into nobody but the hotel maid. She was vacuuming the lobby rug. I had left the fish sack in the trunk of the Porsche and I'd had the good sense to leave my bird book in the car as well. I wasn't smelling like any bird watcher.

"Mornin'," the maid said.

That's country where nothing is wasted and that includes words. Maybe you were being wished a good morning but the thought could be that it's good if a man gets to have any morning at all.

"Good morning, Day," I said.

Everybody called her Day because her name was Marguerite and marguerites are daisies and Day was short for Daisy. They're people who don't even waste syllables.

"Been fishing?" she said.

If you're thinking that when you go fishing you don't catch fish that have been long dead, remember fishing boats. If they aren't sluiced down frequently and thoroughly, they do carry on them the obtrusive memories of catches long gone. Also fishing is done at night or so early in the morning that it makes no difference.

I gave it the rueful smile.

"I was hoping I smelled like I'd been out picking roses," I said.

Laughing, she hit the switch of the vacuum cleaner. It wasn't as noisy as the tide coming up the gorge, but it was noisy enough to knock off further conversation and that was all right with me.

I went up to the room and shucked out of my clothes. With special care for the leather button I emptied my pockets. The clothes I left in a heap on top of the dresser. Day would see to getting them out to a cleaner. If he didn't have the magic for getting them defished, I could always burn them.

Myself I took under the shower. It was a long shower, much suds repeated many times over and much shampooing. By the time I was ready to come out from under it and towel off, I was smelling of nothing, not even of myself, just of soap.

While I shaved, I congratulated myself on having come out of it with no marks on me that clothes wouldn't cover up. Nothing but the place on my thumb where the blackberry thorn had stabbed me and that wasn't conspicuous. On examination I could see it, but that was only because I knew it was there and I did inspect. Nobody else would ever notice it.

The rest of me, most of those parts that I was going to keep under the cover of clothes, was marked but good. Surveying the bright red lines of abrasion and the black and blue and green and yellow areas of contusion plus those purple passages where contusion merged with abrasion, I felt that I could compete color for color with even the most luridly illustrated of the Leather Vests I'd seen out front of the drugstore. I could have passed for the masterpiece of some Abstract Expressionist tattoo artist. I looked like I'd been action-painted.

When I came out of the bathroom, the clothes I'd left piled on the dresser were gone. The bed had been made and the room had been cleaned. Since I had been early up, Day had done the obvious. She had come in and gotten a jump on her morning's work. She was a good maid, efficient, thorough, and a demon for work. Her cleaning was so formidable that dirt went off in terrified flight at her approach. With the bathroom door shut and the shower running loud around my ears, I had, of course, not heard her vacuum cleaner when she was doing the room. She, on the other hand, would certainly have heard the shower going and, when she had finished the room, she had gone off, leaving the bathroom to do later.

Without being told, she was getting my stuff to the cleaner. It was no more than I might have expected. It was the way she operated. I pulled out the dresser drawer where I had shorts and socks and then for a time I forgot what I'd gone there for.

On the dresser top was all my pocket stuff, lying just as I'd left it. Change, billfold, keys, pen, pencil, notebook, pocket knife. Only one thing was gone from there and that was the leather button. It was round, of course, and I had a quick vision of it rolling off the dresser top and being sucked up off the floor by Day's vacuum cleaner.

But it wasn't that round. The irregularities of its woven surface would be some impediment to rolling and I remembered how I had left it. I had been careful of it. Just on the chance of its rolling, I had fenced it around.

Maybe I wouldn't have been so certain of what I was remembering if the fence I had built hadn't still been there just as I'd set it up. Billfold, key case, notebook, and pocket knife were set to form a small square and it had been in that square space in their midst that I had set down the button. Nothing else had been disturbed. Only the button, and it had been lifted out of my square.

It had to be that Day had it and this was something I didn't like. In my experience of her since I'd been at the hotel, I would have sworn for her honesty. That she would lift anything was inconceivable. I had no count on the change I'd left on the dresser top alongside my neat little square and only a rough idea of how much of the folding stuff I'd had in the billfold. I counted the change. If she had taken any of that, it couldn't have been much. I counted the bills. There were a few more of those than I would have said on my rough guess.

It seemed most unlikely that she could have touched either, but why the button? What could she want with that? I couldn't think, or, if I could, I didn't want to.

It was no good standing there and scowling at the empty square. I hauled out the shorts and socks and slammed the drawer shut. I hauled a second drawer open and took out a shirt. Then I slammed that one shut. I felt like slamming things, but all my slamming was doing nothing for me. I went on feeling that way.

Growling at myself, I pulled the shorts on and then moved over to the easy chair to pull on the socks. As soon as I hit the chair, I saw it. Alongside the chair was a small table that held a lamp and an ash tray. In the clean ash tray sat the button. I felt better, but not good—only better.

Knowing Day and the way she went about any job of cleaning and tidying up, I could reconstruct it. She had picked up the clothes and taken them out of the room to send them off for cleaning but she would never have stopped at that. She wouldn't leave the dresser top without dusting it.

That would mean that she carefully picked up the pocket junk, dusted under it, and put it back exactly as I had left it. She just hadn't put the button back the way I'd had it. Knowing Day, I thought I could reconstruct that as well.

This was a female with a low opinion of males. Men were creatures who could never be counted on to do anything right. They were sloppy and they were careless. A round button hanging about loose could roll away and get itself lost. Manlike I had protected this button from rolling but I'd done it in the half-assed way men always did things.

Day had known what was going to happen. Erridge was going to come out of the shower and start getting himself dressed. He'd scoop up his pocket stuff to stow it back in his pockets. The button was likely to roll and if, when it did, he had already scooped up any part of that hedge he had built around it, it was all too likely to roll off on to the floor and lose itself. She had just given it the woman's touch, taking it from the dresser top and putting it in the ash tray where it was permanently hedged around and properly safe.

So I felt better, but I couldn't get it out of my head that she had seen it. She had handled it. It was a good bet she would remember it, and that I couldn't like.

I pulled on my socks and climbed into my shirt. Buttoning it, I was satisfied that for the upper part of me it covered all my Abstract Expressionist decorations. Slacks would take care of covering the rest. I went to the closet for a pair of those. The ones I wanted were hanging under a jacket and I knew just where they were. I reached for them and they weren't there. That made me look at what I was doing. The jacket on the hanger I'd reached for had no slacks hanging under it. It had none because the ones that ordinarily would have been there were the ones I'd been wearing, the pair that had gone off for cleaning. The slacks I was looking for were where they should have been, hanging under the jacket I usually wore with them, but the hangers had been switched. The one I wanted had been moved from the right-hand end of the row to the left-hand end.

I could think of no way for figuring that and I tried to think it didn't matter. There was no conceivable way I could bring to mind that would make it matter, but, all the same, I couldn't put it out of my head. It had to mean something and I was bugged with the thought that I needed to know what.

I finished dressing, but that I did mechanically. My mind wasn't on it. I was trying to think and the more I worked at it, the more I was coming up baffled and confused. Between the moment when I was knocked out and my return to the hotel there had been a good piece of time. It could have been more than enough for anybody who had been interested to sneak into my room and go through my things.

But why? A thief? I took time out from getting my clothes on and took inventory. There hadn't been anything in the room except my clothes and a couple of empty suitcases. Except for this switch in the position of clothes hangers there was no indication that anyone had been at my stuff. The button had been moved, but that could have been no one but Day. During all the time I'd been pulling myself together and getting myself up out of the gorge the button had been with me. All the things that had been in the room while I was out in the fog were still there. Nothing had been taken. It would need to have been a disappointed thief. He'd found nothing he thought worth taking.

So what thief? The guy who blipped me and tied me up in the sack? It could be if you wanted to think crazy. On second thought, however, how could it be? He hadn't just disposed of me and buzzed off. He'd been there later to pitch the motorcycle down into the rapids and that took care of his time. Between disposing of Erridge and disposing of the motorcycle he could never have made it. That had been too short a piece of time.

One bucko eliminated Erridge and another eliminated the motorcycle? Multiply them and anything becomes possible. I could even make it a third one who worked my hotel room while his buddies busied themselves out in the fog. If the multiplication made it more possible, it also made it less believable. Set it up as the work of one man and it made no sense. Set it up as a gang operation and it made less than no sense. Less than nothing? Why not? You've never heard of minus quantities, Charlie?

There was no way I could think about it that didn't bring

me back to Day. She had taken the button from the dresser and put it in the ash tray. She had also been into the closet examining stuff. Once she had been sending a load out for cleaning, she had looked the closet stuff over just in case there might be something else that would need it.

Trying it every which way, I convinced myself that I couldn't do better than that. It was the most reasonable explanation. The only thing I could see wrong with it was that it was also the explanation I wanted to believe. I kept asking myself whether it couldn't be that my wanting to believe it was a big part of its seeming so reasonable. I kept pushing the question away. I'm a hard-nosed, hard-headed, practical engineer. Wishful thinking isn't my bag. At least I like to believe it isn't.

I finished dressing, while I was doing it, I was hearing Day's vacuum cleaner growl its way over the floor of the upstairs hall. When I came out of the room, she was still there pushing it around. She switched it off.

"I got all that stuff out for you," she said. "It was smelling up the room."

"Yes. I noticed. Thanks."

"The pants'll need cleaning. The rest can go in the wash."

"You'll take care of it?"

"If you want."

"I'd appreciate it."

"No trouble."

I sent up a trial balloon.

"Did you see anything else you'd say needs doing?" I asked.

"Nothing."

"Once those things are going out, did you look?"

"You got anything else you want to go, give it to me," she said, returning to her vacuuming.

I had taken all the time she was prepared to give me. She had her work to do. Just in case she hadn't made it clear enough, she drove it home. She ran the cleaner around me in tight circles. If I would take myself downstairs where I belonged, she could get the whole floor done.

I went down to breakfast. The dining room had only just opened up and Erridge was the first one in. Breakfasts in that hotel were geared to the needs of farmers and fishermen, hard workers who never tied on the feed bag until after they'd been up for hours either doing the morning chores or hauling in the nets or the lobster pots. When they came to table, they had their eating shoes on. This was one morning when Erridge could compete. He could meet the hungriest man in the state fork to fork.

I took all of it and I was still packing it away when Jack Humphrey came down and joined me. He was yawning and stretching and rubbing sleep out of his eyes. He looked at the food I was wolfing down and he winced.

"How's to let me go into you for a cup of coffee out of your pot?" he groaned. "Pay you back when they bring me mine, but I don't think I can wait."

I passed him the coffeepot.

"Help yourself," I said. "More here than I could ever soak up. It would keep me awake all morning."

He poured himself a cup and the way his hand was shaking I thought I should have poured it for him. Looking reproachfully at his hand, he tried to make it behave itself. It did steady enough to lift the cup to his mouth. He drank it down, black and scalding.

"Whew," he said.

Maybe it was relief and maybe it was agony. There was no way of knowing.

"Asbestos lips?" I asked.

"Maybe I'll know by afternoon. You ever tangled with Medford rum?"

It seemed like the wrong morning for that question. Up in those parts, I think I told you, Sunday is a dry day, no bars open anywhere. I could have asked him where he found all that rum of a Sunday night, but that was his business. If he'd located a blind pig and wanted to tell me about it, he could.

"I've had it but never in a big way," I said.

"Then you don't know. Any time you get drinking around here, watch it, brother. It's all right for the natives. They've developed immunities or something. Me, I've been trampled by a parade of elephants."

"Tie one on last night?"

"More like I had one tied on me."

"Night on the town with the illustrated skins?"

He started to shake his head but he quickly thought better of it. You know those mornings when everything has come loose and painful inside your skull? Mornings like that heads are in no shape for shaking. You want to hold still in the hope that things will stop jumping up and down on the rear walls of your eyeballs.

"They drink beer," he said. "A shot of rye when they can get it, but mostly it's beer."

"Then who are the rummies?" I asked.

"They're not rummies. They're the best people, the pillars of society, the big shots, the gentlemen who call all the turns."

He explained and it seemed to be like locking horns with the Russians. I've heard tell that fellows in our Moscow embassy in preparation for any kind of social do with the Kremlin crowd take on a load of gut insulation. Some eat a big slog of butter and some swig a healthy slug of olive oil. Either one is supposed to make the vodka keep its distance even when you've got it down inside you. Without the butter or the oil a diplomat can find himself coming down with an undiplomatic case of loosened tongue.

The way Humph told it, that was what had happened to him. It wasn't vodka, of course, but it was the rum and he had gone into it naked of insulation. He was a little vague about details but the general picture was hospitality Kremlin style. He knew his host, one E. E. Coffin.

Up in those parts you'll run into Coffins all over the place. It's Coffin country. They outnumber the Smiths and the Joneses, but even I knew that E. E. Coffin wasn't just any old member of the increased tribe. This was Edward Ebenezer Coffin and Edward Ebenezer was Mr. Big. You'd have to go up or down that coast for what the natives would call a "far piece" before you'd come up against another Mr. Big who pulled even half the weight pulled by Edward Ebenezer.

His house was the largest for miles around. It was also the oldest. The way it was kept up it looked like the newest but only if you weren't noticing stuff like handmade window glass and hand-wrought hinges and lock plates. I had picked up enough local lore to know that it had been built by a Coffin more than two hundred years back and nobody but Coffins had ever lived in it, even if, as now, it was only the one Coffin. Edward Ebenezer lived there alone.

It hadn't been just the two of them. For all the fuzziness of his remembering, Humph did recall the mayor and also mayors of other towns along the coast. It was his impression that the mayors had been backed up by bank presidents and others such.

"These guys are operators," he said. "They're smooth. They're slick. They're polite. Boy, are they polite!"

The way he was remembering it, they took him one at a time. It was all done with that beautiful, old-fashioned courtesy. Here was a large gathering of important men and they were all eager to get to know Jack Humphrey and to make Jack Humphrey feel at home, all working to put him at his ease and make him feel he was one of them.

"They passed me from hand to hand," he said, "and every

one of them had his shot at hoisting the rum with me. Get it?"

"They spelled each other," I said, "and you had nobody there to spell you."

"I had a ball," he moaned, "and now I'm hungover."

He waved a hand to indicate how far he was hungover. I gathered it was something like all the way to the outer limits of the continental shelf.

"And your hangover is the least of what's bugging you," I said.

"Hangovers come and hangovers go," he mourned. "I'll get over this one. I'll get well even though right now I could think I never will. What's killing me is what I must have said. I talked. I know I talked. It's a cinch I said plenty even if I can't remember what. One or another of them, they got what they wanted. There was never much hope I'd get them sold. I knew that before I ever came up here, but all the same . . . I didn't have to go and blow it."

I tried to tell him that maybe he was exaggerating. We've all had these mornings when we'd like to remember, when just the fact that we can't remember seems like sure-shot proof that there has to be something we need to remember, something disastrous. Freud to the contrary notwithstanding, more often than not there's been nothing.

"For all you know," I said, "you didn't say one damn thing that mattered and, even if you did, you can always fall back on how you haven't got their head for rum. Whatever they come up with, you just tell them it was the rum talking. Nothing to it."

"They won't come up with anything," Humph predicted. "Not with me, they won't. They're just storing it away and making their minds up on it."

It figured. I couldn't say it didn't. They'd given him the treatment and, when they were ready to act, they would act and that would be as smooth and as slick as their investigation had been. Over my breakfast I'd come halfway around toward deciding to go to the fuzz after all. Day had seen the button. Though she had always been close-mouthed with me, I couldn't be certain of her. Would she be close-mouthed with her friends and neighbors, the folks she had known all her life? I knew her full name. It was Marguerite Ruisseau.

How's your French, Charlie? I'll save you looking it up. A ruisseau is a brook. So they'd christened her Marguerite. You wouldn't expect that they'd have named her Babbling, but it was something to think about and I'd been thinking.

But then poor old Humph had come along and poured his lamentations all over my thinking and I switched right back to where I'd been. Maybe I hadn't imagined that it would be anything so slick and so smoothly organized, but I had known that I would get myself worked over. It seemed as though I'd do better to take my chances on Day. She'd seen the button and she'd moved it from where I'd left it to what she considered a safer place. That didn't mean she would know the significance of the thing. How could she know?

Meanwhile Humph had been discovering that he could manage food. Not much, but some. He was taking it down and holding it down and it seemed to be helping his hang-over even if it was doing nothing for his depression. I was busy with my own thoughts when he startled me out of them with a sudden laugh. It was one of the bitter variety laughs, the kind a man dips in gall so he can use it for punishing himself.

"There was one guy didn't get there last night," he said. "He was supposed to come. They expected him, but he never showed. It bothered them a lot. They kept talking about it. 'Where's Sam Ellsworth? This isn't at all like Sam. Anybody you can rely on, it's Sam Ellsworth. He says he's going to come, he comes. What could have happened to him?' They went on and on about him. They called his

house and they were told he wasn't home. He had gone to
E. E. Coffin's. They worried. They talked about driving in
the fog. Something had to have happened to good, reliable,
old Sam. Like they were thinking there weren't enough of
them for pouring the rum into me."

I grabbed at that. The guy needed bucking up and I got
in there and bucked.

"See," I told him. "It's not nearly as bad as you've been
thinking. It's not like you're drawing a blank. You remember
that. If you don't remember what you might have said, it's
likely there's nothing to remember. It can be you said nothing."

He was hanging on to his misery. He wouldn't be pried
loose from it.

"That's not all I remember," he said. "I remember I
talked. I talked and I talked. All I can't remember is what I
said."

We left the dining room together. Passing along the hall,
Humph found fresh salt to rub into his wounds. The walls of
that hall were lined with framed photographs. They were
pictures of boats and pictures of the crews that had raced
them. You could read those pictures for a complete history
of the local regattas. The oldest ones were faded sepia prints
where all the yachtsmen looked like William Howard Tafts
in yachting caps. The later ones were sharp color prints.
Early or late, they were all labeled with names of boats and
names of the men who crewed them.

My moaning masochist ignored the old-time ones. He
went along the line of the color prints turning the screw on
himself. He found E. E. Coffin in a flock of them and with
him no few of the companions of the night before. Jabbing
his finger at them, he picked them out for me.

"He was there," he said. "And so was he and he and he."

While he was busy assembling a full roll call of his inquis-
itors, he lost me. I spotted a picture of the man who wasn't

there, Samuel Coffin Ellsworth. It had to be good, reliable, old Sam and not only because this was a Sam Ellsworth who was evidently a member of the club. I knew him on sight even before I read his label.

Along with his yachting cap and the modest but pleased grin of the winner, the color photography had done a great job of recording his beautiful sports jacket. You know those old portraits, the kind for which the sitter would get dressed up in his best clothes and the artist worked as hard at getting a likeness of the threads as he did on the likeness of the sitter himself?

The photographer had done just that kind of a job on Samuel Coffin Ellsworth, on his yachting cap, and on the jacket that looked as though it had been woven out of threads of crème Chantilly. The color of it hit me and the luxurious-looking softness. Also in that line of pictures that jacket was an eccentricity. Everyone else along the line was wearing the conventional blazer with the conventional glitter of brass buttons or else one of those rugged turtleneck pullovers a woman knits in the west of Ireland so that when her man drowns and his unrecognizable body is washed ashore she can know him by her knitting.

So Samuel Coffin Ellsworth was the standout. His was the only jacket of that color and that softness, and the camera had caught every one of the leather buttons he'd had on it. I put that in the past because at least one of those buttons wasn't on the jacket any more. Erridge had it in his pocket.

I left Jack Humphrey to his painful researches. He didn't need me. He could nurse his misery without me and I had places to go. I didn't know what I was going to do in those places, but I was going to think about that along the way.

There was a phone booth out in the lobby and a local phone book. I looked up Ellsworths and had a sinking moment when I was confronted with a full page of them. Even the Samuel Ellsworths looked to be uncomfortably numer-

ous, but it wasn't as bad as it looked. I tried for a Samuel C.
and I was rewarded with something even better. He was
listed under his full name, Samuel Coffin Ellsworth. If a cat
had a Coffin, he flaunted it.

He was listed for a town down the coast, about thirty
miles to the south. That was no problem. Baby was standing
where I'd left her out front and the sun was standing high
and strong. It had eaten up the fog as efficiently as Erridge
had cleaned up his breakfast. One time or another I was
going to have to tool down there for a look at the way the
tide behaved in those parts and I could be there in more
than enough time for picking me a good spot from which I
could watch the afternoon turning.

I'd be mixing business and business even though I hadn't
even begun to figure what I had that I could put into the
mix. Do you walk into a man's house cold and ask him if he's
got all his buttons? Or is it going to be Erridge's Boy Scout
deed for the day? I found this here now button, Mister, and
I thought as how it might be yours, so I drove thirty miles
just on the chance that you'd be looking for it.

Where did I find it? No problem there. On a ledge in the
gorge. I didn't have to say when. I didn't have to say it was
in the fish sack. Driving along, I hauled it out of my pocket
and smelled it. It was okay. Either the leather hadn't picked
up the fish stink or the smell had evaporated off it. The
fuzzy bit was carrying a little of the smell but it was such a
small scrap of fuzz that it couldn't hold much. Only by
working my nose hard could I detect it and even then I
wasn't sure that I was smelling it or only thinking I was because I knew the fragrance ought to be there.

It was a good drive. That's beautiful country up there and
under the morning sun it was looking its best. Trees, grass,
shrubs, everything that was green had been freshened by its
soak in the fog. Under the sun the whole countryside looked

as though people had been up all night polishing it, rubbing up every leaf and every blade of grass to a brilliant sheen.

Samuel Coffin Ellsworth's town was small, a one-street community that differed from the surrounding country only in that for a short stretch along the road the houses stood closer together, surrounding themselves only with gardens, lawns, vegetable patches, and small orchards—no barns, no fields, no meadows. There was a small white church, a small red town hall, and a general store that was also the post office. If I had been giving the Porsche her head, I could have been through the town and out the other side of it without ever having noticed I was there.

I took it slowly, reading the names on the mail boxes that stood at the road edge. I had expected a large house and a fine one. I had seen the photograph and had automatically come up with the expectations that went with the Ellsworth jacket and the Ellsworth boat. An Ellsworth who did himself as well in those departments as this Sam did would hardly be likely to house himself in a hovel.

Biggest and most impressive house in town? It was a good enough hunch but, rolling along past those houses, I could see that it wasn't going to be any help. All the houses were big and all were imposing. I had to depend wholly on the mail boxes but that was all right. One did come up and it had the full name lettered on its side.

I had gone nowhere toward deciding what my approach could be, but I didn't need it. Behind that mail box in the well-raked gravel driveway stood what looked to be everything I might need. It was a car, but no ordinary car. It bounced the sunlight off its every surface in so bright a dazzle that I had to blink some of the glare of it out of my eyes before I could see it properly.

It was a Stutz Bearcat and it could have been the shining star of any antique car museum. It was one of the great old ones but it didn't look old. It looked as though through every one of its venerable years it had been tuned and buffed and polished so that age could not wither nor custom stale. Alongside that great veteran my Porsche had to look like a kid, but just on condition Baby and the Bearcat could have been of an age.

Where it wasn't polished brass it was beautiful creamy enamel and rich, creamy leather. It had to be Samuel Coffin Ellsworth's car. If it posed any question, it would have been whether Sam had had it painted and upholstered to match his great jacket or had had the jacket made to match his Stutz.

I knew a gal once who was in the couturier racket. Her prize customer every year sent her cuttings of the hair of her pet pooch so that when my friend made up that season's sets of threads for the lady, they would match the pup. I was given to understand that similar cuttings of dog hair went to Detroit each year so that each year's Cadillac would also match up. The way I've always visualized it, there was this mutt who rode around on a lap and the lap was in a Caddy and both the lap and the Caddy matched what the dog had been before he got snatched bald to provide all those cuttings.

I let myself wonder whether here there mightn't also be a dog in the picture, but I put the thought aside as unimportant. I had my approach. I drive by in the Porsche and I see the Stutz. Could I just drive by? Wouldn't it be necessary, inevitable, polite, and what-have-you to stop, to ring the doorbell, to say a few words of appreciation? Surely the situation called for a salute from the great present to the great past. It certainly was going to do for starters.

I parked the Porsche and walked up the driveway. Once I was past the Bearcat I could put my mind on the house. It was big, not quite as big as the imposing Coffin job I've already told you about, but still a lot of house. It wasn't as old either. It had maybe a hundred years back of it as against the two centuries and more of the other job, but it was also beautifully kept up. It had a big bay window bellying out toward the lawn in front. There were no curtains. It was a window that asked you to look in and what you saw there was nothing anyone could be living in.

It was a show window. It had on display some hooked rugs, patchwork quilts, painted tin weathervanes, old hand-blown glass bottles, duck decoys, full-rigged ship models with sails made of log paper gone brown with age, bits of scrimshaw, some silver, some pewter.

The window made it even easier. It said that Samuel Coffin Ellsworth was running an antique shop in his old family home. It was one of those supremely genteel antique shops, nothing so vulgar as a sign in the window or a shingle out by the road, but the window display was there to let the passing tourist know that customers would be welcome. If you know New England, you know antique dealers of this kind. They've gone into trade but only with discreet reticence. If you've done any pricing, you also know that you're expected to pay for the discretion and the reticence.

The front door stood open. Sam Ellsworth had evidently raided his stock for something to hold it open. The improvised doorstop was a kid's cast-iron bank in the shape of Uncle Sam with the coin slot in the top of his tall hat.

The whole setup said "walk in," but I was feeling my way. I pushed the doorbell. I was rewarded beyond any man's wildest expectations. Out of the shadowed reaches within popped a girl. Don't ask me to describe her. I haven't the words. Maybe I can give you an idea. There's a place in *The Iliad* where old Homer had the problem. What do you do about the beauty of Helen of Troy? How do you describe the indescribable? The way Homer did it, he has the old men of Troy taking the sun on the ramparts of the city walls. They're moaning and griping about the war, talking up its losses and its horrors. Then Helen comes out and walks past and the old boys look at her and they say it's all been worth it.

So let me do it the way Homer did. At my first glimpse of this Peachcake I could run through my mind the stink of the fish sack, the way I'd missed death by only a whisker, all the bruises and scratches and lumps I was hauling around under my shirt and my slacks. I added them all up and I looked at this apparition. The apparition smiled at me and in my heart I was saying with those old Trojans it's all been worth it.

"Come in," she said. "Come in and look around."

"I'm looking," I said. "Will I see anything as beautiful inside?"

The way she fielded that one showed right off that she had all the skills of a great and experienced glove. It stood to reason. A girl can't go around looking the way she did without drawing from every cat that comes by some show of gallantry. She probably didn't even know what men looked like when they weren't bug-eyed and panting.

"I saw you in the driveway when you were looking at the Stutz," she said. "She is a beauty, isn't she? But then you're not doing badly for wheels yourself. That's a Porsche, isn't it?"

"Right," I said, "and she used to be the love of my life."

"Forget it," she laughed. "Mr. Ellsworth will never be persuaded to sell the Stutz."

I stepped inside. She led the way to the room behind the bay window. It ran to form, the shop that wasn't quite a shop. It was all set up like somebody's room and it looked the part as long as you didn't think of what it would be like to live in it. It couldn't be done. It would be you or the things and never enough room for both.

"Is Mr. Ellsworth around?" I asked.

She came up with a look of worry that packed her smile away. It could even have been a look of panic.

"No," she said. "He isn't and he should be. I can't think what's happened to him. I do hope he's all right but it does seem as though he should have telephoned."

"You're frightened," I said.

"I know it's silly of me." She was looking for her smile and not finding it. "But some people are all right on motorcycles. They give you the feeling they can handle it, no matter what. But he isn't at all good at it. Just seeing him on it puts your heart in your mouth and, if anyone should wear a helmet, he should and he won't, not ever."

"He's gone off somewhere on his motorcycle?"

She shrugged.

"He isn't here and it isn't here," she said, "and he hasn't telephoned and Sarah—she keeps house for him—Sarah says he hasn't been here all night. I knew where he was supposed to be yesterday evening and I've called there. They've been worried because he never came. So where is he?"

I went back out to the door for another look at the Stutz. She was dry and not a stain or blemish on her anywhere.

"Sarah's mistaken," I said. "He must have been here some time this morning. It has to have been after the fog burned off. The Bearcat wasn't out in the drive all night. Look at it. You can see it was under cover, protected from the fog. It was moved out after the fog lifted."

She shook her head.

"I moved it," she said.

She explained. Although the car wasn't for sale and it never would be, it did have its place in the business. It was a come-on. People driving by saw it in the driveway. They stopped and looked at it and, once stopped, they saw the bay window with its display of antique stuff. They came in. It worked better than a sign.

"Any time the weather permits," she said, "he moves it out of the garage first thing in the morning. Any time the weather turns sour it goes in and every evening it goes in. When I got here this morning and it wasn't out and he wasn't here, I moved it out. I always do when he isn't around to do it himself."

"I see," I said.

I wasn't about to give her any rundown on all that I was seeing, the button, the motorcycle, the fish sack. When the motorcycle came hurtling past me, it had come bouncing down solo. No rider came tumbling with it or after it. I was certain of that.

She pulled herself together. She even found her smile and turned it on me.

"Did you have an appointment with Mr. Ellsworth?" she asked.

"Oh no. No appointment."

That was a relief to her. Obviously if he'd had an appointment and hadn't shown for it, it would have been something to add to her worry.

"But you did want to see him? I won't do?"

The last thing in the world I could ever have brought myself to say to this girl would be that she wouldn't do.

"I did want to see him," I said.

"I'm awfully sorry," she murmured. "I'll tell him you called. If you'll leave your name and where he can reach you."

I gave her my name and told her where I was staying. The smile went off and got lost again.

"That's where he was supposed to be last night," she said. "Not the hotel but just down the street from it. You didn't see him last night by any chance?"

"No," I said. "I didn't see him."

She looked as though she might be wondering whether she could believe me. She was scared. She was convinced that there was something going on and now she'd begun to think I might be a part of it.

"This is all so strange," she said. "Not at all like Mr. Ellsworth."

"I'll come by later," I said, "or I'll phone. Who do I ask for?"

"Mr. Ellsworth. Sam Ellsworth."

"I mean if he isn't back, if I want to talk to you."

"It's likely I'll be answering the phone if it isn't Mr. Ellsworth, but it's Rachel—Rachel Freeman."

She walked out to the Porsche with me and I gave myself up to enjoying every step of that short walk. I wished I hadn't parked so close. I had the depressing thought that in all likelihood these were to be the only moments of her company I was ever going to get to enjoy.

I didn't know what was going on with her boss or her boy friend or whatever Samuel Coffin Ellsworth might have been to her, but something was going on. Whether I would be staying out of it or even could stay out of it remained to be seen, but staying out would probably mean staying away and not ever seeing her again. Getting involved, on the other hand, showed every sign of being worse. I was telling her nothing and if she ever got to know as much, she was not going to like me for it.

But she did like Baby. She walked around her and there was nothing ignorant about her appreciation. This girl, Rachel, knew her wheels.

"Do you ever let anyone else drive her?" she asked.

"Not often," I said.

"Of course, not. If she were mine, I'd be so jealous of her, I'd never let anyone else even touch her."

"If anyone is beautiful enough," I said, "anyone can touch her. If anyone knows enough about driving, it could be arranged."

"I'd love to sometime," she said. "Just for a few minutes, just to get the feel."

"Now?"

She was tempted, but only tempted. She resisted it.

"You're sweet," she said, "but no. Not now. People do stop by and Sarah's no good with customers. Also I do want to stay by the phone."

There was nothing for it but pulling out in a cloud of platitudes. If anything bad had happened, you'd have heard. Bad news travels fast. No news is good news. The lot.

IV

You may remember that I'd had some notion of hanging on down that way and mixing business with business. I gave up the idea. Looking at the tide run along that stretch of the coast could wait for another day. There was something else I wanted to look at and I couldn't wait with that. It was bugging me.

I drove back the way I'd come and, stopping in at the hotel, I went up to my room. Before I'd gone down to breakfast I'd done something there and I was taking a moment to check it out.

I'd stuck a burnt-out match stick between the closet door and the door jamb. It hadn't been any good fixing one in the door to the room. Day would have been coming in to finish up in there. She'd still had my bathroom to do, so I wouldn't have needed anything like that to tell me whether she'd been in or not. That much I'd know from the scrubbed floor and the fresh towels.

I wanted to know whether she or anyone had been back to my closet. I opened the door and the matchstick dropped. That left me with a tougher question. It could mean that nobody had been to the closet, but it could also mean that someone had seen the matchstick and had known what it was there for and that it had been put back when the closet door was closed. The trick wasn't that new. Everybody watches television. Everybody sees movies.

For what it might be worth, though, I set it up again and this time I had another matchstick for the door to the room.

She'd been in. She'd scrubbed up the bathroom and left me the fresh towels and fresh soap. When I came back downstairs lunch was on. Having been first in for breakfast, my gut was letting me know that it was ready for lunch, but it wasn't yelling for it. The breakfast I'd taken aboard should have been enough to last me the whole day, but I wasn't going to ask that much of it. It was just going to last me a little while longer. I didn't need to be the first man in for lunch.

Now I tried to do what I should have done in the first place. The thinking I'd done at daybreak hadn't been any good. Making the choice of not tipping my hand, I hadn't considered the obvious, the good chance that it might be tipped for me. Somebody takes a good shot at trying to bump me off and I'm so business-as-usual that I choose to keep it personal. I don't go to the police.

How's that going to look when the thing does come out in the open? It's going to look like Erridge played it sneaky and that's no way for a man to look when he has a project to sell. When you're trying to sell an idea, the thing you need most is creditability and playing it cozy wasn't going to win me any of that.

Maybe at first I did have the notion that I could keep it under wraps and handle it myself. I went down to see Sam Ellsworth with just that in mind. So Ellsworth was missing and his motorcycle was missing and I had information I couldn't hold out.

I went around to the police station. There was nobody there but one kid cop. I told him I had something I wanted to report, an assault.

"Who was hit?"

"I was."

He looked me over. What he saw evidently didn't grab him. I could have taken my shirt off and let him have a look at the evidence but it was too obvious that anything I might

do with him would just have to be done over again with
somebody who mattered.

"You all right?" he asked. "You look all right."

"I'm all right."

"Everybody's eating dinner. Come back after dinner."

I should have left my name, but he didn't ask for it. I let
it go.

I took the road I'd taken the night before, but now I
could let Baby roll. We had a dry road and no fog to slow us
down. There was going to be no better time for doing what
I had in mind. It was just out of habit that I'd called it
lunch. I knew it was dinner. This was noontime-dinner
country. Breakfast, dinner, and supper is the feeding sched-
ule around there and dinner is taken seriously. There's the
one hour in the middle of the day when everything stops.
Everybody has moved indoors and is busy stoking up. I was
counting on having the road turnout by the gorge all to myself.

I wasn't planning on doing anything much. I just wanted
to have a look at where I'd been the night before. I
wanted to see it by daylight, the spot where the motorcycle
had been parked, the level at which I'd been knocked out,
the ledge on which I'd come to. I had seen it before. I'd explored it before. I knew it well.

I wanted to know if anything had changed there since last
I'd seen it by daylight. I knew that there could have been
small changes I wouldn't be able to detect. I wasn't
prepared to account for every last twig or every patch of
moss, but it was possible that there might be something I
could see. In any event, I felt I had to look and, since it
would mean looking carefully, I preferred to do it unob-
served.

The road turnout was a disappointment. It wasn't empty.
In my thoughts about dinnertime I had omitted a factor from
my calculations. I had forgotten picnics. A Ford station-

wagon stood in the turnout. Alongside it at a folding table on a pair of folding chairs were two people. The wagon wore Nebraska plates. The people were an old woman and an old man and they wore Nebraska faces. You know those HOME-FOR-THANKSGIVING calendar pictures, Charlie? They were the grandma and grandpop the people in those pictures come home to.

They were enjoying the view of the gorge and the rapids while they tucked into their sandwiches and milk and apples and cheese. When I pulled up they divided their enjoyment between gorge and rapids and the Porsche and me.

They said "hello" and I said "hello" right back at them.

"That's a sight down there," the old man said.

"Nothing like Nebraska."

"Nothing like anything we've ever seen," the old lady marveled. "That's a river down there. It's a river on the map and it looks like a river, but it smells like salt water. How can that be?"

"For a good way up it's tidal," I explained. "It's salt when the tide comes in. "It's ebb now, so it's fresh, but even between tides the smell of salt hangs on. Pools of sea water stay behind on the rocks alongside the rapids and the mosses down there are soaked with it."

"You live around here?" the old man asked.

"No, but I'm staying a while."

"Nice place to be staying." He turned his attention to Baby. "That's one of them foreign cars," he said.

It sounded like an accusation. I confessed to Baby's immigrant status.

"Looks like she can go," he commented.

I told him that she could go. So then he wanted to know all the usual things. How many miles on a gallon, how fast she could go, the fastest I'd ever done in her, what a car like that costs.

They were nice old folks. She wanted me to have a sandwich or an apple or whatever, but I said something about not wanting to spoil my dinner. It was the right thing to say. It struck that sympathetic chord, gave her a picture of someone like herself who would be doing prodigious things over a hot stove in preparation for tying the feed bag on Erridge.

I excused myself. I didn't try to explain what I was doing. I just climbed over the guardrail and took myself out of sight around the blackberry thicket. I'd been hoping there would be something showing there, a spot or two of oil or possibly a tire track in a mossy area on the rock ledge.

It was too high for moss and the bare rock showed nothing. I climbed on down, watching for anything I might spot on the way. So far as I could see, everything was as it always had been. I located the place where I'd taken the hit but I did it only by memory. There was nothing there to mark the spot. Down at that level there were mosses, but none of them looked scraped or gouged.

If I would have liked to think I had put up a fight even though I had no memory of it, there was nothing to indicate that I had even shuffled my feet. I went on down to the ledge where I'd made my landing, but that was a futile effort. I couldn't expect to find anything there. The tide had begun sweeping it clean even before I had managed to pull myself up off it. Since then it had been scoured by the full force of the water. Anything that might have been there would have been carried away. Any marks would have been erased.

I looked up and I did see what I hadn't been able to see from above or while I'd been climbing. The scars left by the tumbling motorcycle did show on the rock face. They weren't anything much and they were hardly conspicuous. I could see them because I knew they would have to be there and I was looking for them. Up at the top I could see the two old people looking down at me. It was to have been expected. I was an unanticipated floor show for their picnic.

I couldn't make out their faces, but the shine of the sun on their white hair picked them out for me. When I first looked up at them, I had for only a flash an impression that there was a third head up there, someone with them looking down at me. If there had been, however, it seemed to me that he hadn't been enough interested to keep watching, not as interested for instance as were the two old people. He didn't come back for a further look.

I made the climb back up and the old lady greeted me with a sigh of relief.

"I'm glad that's over," she said. "Isn't it dangerous?"

"Not if you've had any experience with climbing," I said. "It's not as hard as it looks."

She shuddered.

"I wouldn't want to try it."

"I wouldn't unless you knew how."

She laughed.

"Never fear," she assured me. "I won't. And while you were risking your neck down there, you missed it. The craziest thing we've seen this whole trip and we've seen crazy things—the Amish in Pennsylvania and the hippies in New York down at the Washington Square, and you can't imagine what all, but this boy beats anything."

"Someone was up here with you?" I asked.

It was easy enough to make it sound like polite interest. She wanted an ear for her travel adventures and I had two ears that were doing nothing else at the time.

"A boy. I suppose a young man. When you get to be our age, until folks have grandchildren they're all girls and boys. We have great-grandchildren."

She was on the edge of sidetracking. A little more and she would be bringing out the pictures of the great-grand-children. If she got that far off it, I wasn't sure I could bring her back to what she'd seen.

"Crazy?" I asked.

"Oh yes. This boy or this young man. He was wearing a leather vest and nothing under it. Just the leather straight against his skin. I don't know, but I think it would be a nasty feeling, but that wasn't all. He's tattooed all over. His arms. His chest. Reminded me of the tattooed lady in the circus, but he was no lady and he wasn't in any circus, just here on the road like anybody ordinary."

"I know," I said. "I've seen them. There's a bunch of them go in for it around here."

I said something polite about nice talking to her and I headed for the Porsche. The old man was over there. When I came up alongside him he took my arm. I was astonished by the strength of his grip. Don't get the idea that he looked feeble. He looked anything but. Nevertheless great-grand-fathers have the right to go just a little soft. It looked as though this old boy hadn't exercised the right. Keeping his voice low, he shot his words at me out of the corner of his mouth.

"I don't want to worry mom or scare her," he said, "so all she's got to know is I'm talking to you about your car. She'll be looking for that. She always says men never talk about nothing but automobiles."

"Something wrong?"

I was going along with him, keeping it low and out of the corner of my mouth.

"You look like a clean, decent young fellow," he said, "and that crazy fool, I didn't like the look of him at all. Greasy and all done up like a painted Indian or something. I thought maybe you should know. You're being followed. That greaseball, he's watching you. Mom didn't catch it. She was too much surprised just by him, the way he looks, to take any notice of how he was acting, but I saw it. The way he took off quick the minute you looked up this way. You say there's a lot of them tattooed like that?"

"Quite a few. I wouldn't know which."

"Unless they're all done alike, I can tell you. He's got all kinds of designs everywhere else, but not his left arm. His left arm all the way up from his hand to his shoulder it's just the one thing. Daisies. Daisies all over, the whole left arm."

"Thanks for telling me. With all those daisies on him, I'll know him if I see him."

"Trouble?" the old man asked. "He looks an ugly customer. Nobody I'd want to turn my back on."

I shrugged it off.

"From what I've seen of them," I said, "they work at looking dangerous. Anybody who works that hard on the look, he's got to be harmless."

"I don't know, mister. I hope you're right, but if there's any way I can help . . ."

"Thanks," I said. "I appreciate it, but there's no problem. It'll turn out he's got nothing on his mind but curiosity. You can figure he's a cat curiosity didn't kill."

I should never have said it. It was no knee-slapper and, as soon as it was out, I could see that the old man was searching around in it for a hidden meaning.

"I don't know," he repeated. "If it hadn't been we were here, I don't know. You climbing around down in there. He could have dropped a rock on you easy."

I promised I'd keep an eye out for the ugly customer. We exchanged names before I took off. Their name was Haskin, Ellen and Henry Haskin, although everybody called them mom and pa, and it had been a pleasure talking to me.

Driving back to the hotel, I watched my rearview mirror. A promise, after all, is a promise and curiosity is curiosity, and you know how it is with us cats.

So the old boy wasn't imagining things. I didn't know about the rock that might have been dropped on me, though on past performance that was a possibility I couldn't very well laugh off, but I was being followed. A motorcycle showed in the mirror. It held too far back for me to pick up any details like a daisy-spangled arm, but I could see the leather vest and what, if I didn't know better, I could have taken for a crazy-printed shirt.

I took Baby down to a walk, holding her to so little speed that it would be out of any motorcycle's range. If you're on only two wheels, there is a minimum velocity below which you cannot remain upright. I thought that way I could force him to come abreast of me and pass me. Anybody who had any knowhow in the tailing game would have done that and then turned off into the first side road to wait till I'd gone past and he could pick up the tail again.

This baby was an amateur and at that maybe a beginner. He stopped and walked his bike for a few moments. Then he picked himself some wildflowers by the side of the road. I assumed they'd be daisies. After all, Charlie, what else?

I pulled up and got out and walked around the Porsche trying to look like a guy who'd come down with a sudden need for checking his tires. My act was as good as his. No better maybe, but as good. I checked the tires. He picked the daisies. We were getting nowhere.

I remounted and gave Baby the gun. If you've ever had anything to do with a Porsche, you know that she's fast off the mark. He jumped for his wheels and I could see him asking that motorcycle for everything it had. That, of course, would never have been enough, not if I'd been about to let Baby show her paces. We could have lost him without ever extending ourselves.

Losing him, however, was the one thing I didn't want to do. The idea was to play him, testing him out. Also there are laws and there are speed traps and it was no time for fooling around with any of those. I had made up my mind to go to the fuzz. I had no yen to do anything that would bring the fuzz to me.

I tried it for only a few seconds and then I brought her down to where she was skimming the top of the legal limit.

Every time I changed my speed, he within his possible limits changed with me. He was following me all the way, but he had established his distance and he worked at keeping it.

If he had turned up at any earlier time, I would have been sure I had him tagged. I've told you how the local line-up went on Jack Humphrey and his oil deal. The Leather Vests were back of him to a tattoo. If Humph had come around to wondering what I was doing with my days and nights, he could easily have enlisted one of the faithful for taking on this job of watching Erridge's movements and coming up maybe with something that would give Humph a clue.

I don't know how much competition there is among oil companies. There are people who will tell you they all work together the world over in a co-operative enterprise of ripping the rest of us off, but we don't have to go into that.

Humph could have been worrying about some other oil outfit moving in to cut him out of the deal even if it was a deal he had little hope of making anyway. On the other hand, he could also be worrying about the sort of thing I was actually studying on. Alternative sources of power. Reduced demand for oil. He'd want to know.

It was still possible. It didn't have to be that the daisy chain in subhuman form was in any way connected with my adventures of the night before or with Samuel Coffin Ellsworth. Certainly I could imagine no way by which Jack Humphrey could be hooked in with any of that.

I didn't know him that well and, just off the top of my head, I would have figured he wasn't the type for playing that rough, but you never can tell. He was in a rough trade. It's a high-stakes game and no holds barred, but the babies that play it are a hard-headed bunch. Maybe they'll do what needs doing and never turn a hair, but I couldn't see where it would ever figure that knocking off Erridge would hit them as something that needed doing. Hell. Even I know

I'm not indispensible. Knock me off and another engineer
will come in and take over on what I'm doing. It would be
waste motion and waste motion is economically unsound.

If these considerations weren't enough for ruling Jack
Humphrey out on the violence jazz, I had the Sam Ellsworth angle. I could see no way of hooking Humphrey
and Ellsworth together. Ellsworth was the guy who never
showed up to do his part in fitting Humph to a hangover. So
where was he all that time? Looking for his lost leather button? And where had he been ever since? What could set a
man to wandering when he had a Peachcake like Rachel
Freeman to come home to?

I drove into town and it was still midday-dinner time.
Traffic was next to nothing and my tail was staying with me
all the way. I passed the hotel without stopping and went on
down to the cove. I parked on the town pier and strolled
along the waterfront. The cove was dotted with boats. Their
sails all neatly furled, they rode out there at anchor.

I was thinking back to the photo of S. C. Ellsworth in the
winners' gallery at the hotel. It was a new picture and I'd
studied its label. It recorded a win in a race that was less
than a year back and it gave the name of his boat. *The Bearcat.* I might not have remembered that but after it had been
topped by the Stutz in the driveway, how could I forget?

I strolled along looking at the boats, thinking I might spot
The Bearcat among them. My tail strolled along looking at
me. So what was he trying to spot? What I was looking for
would be painted the color of cream and it would have
brasswork that would give back the sun in a brighter glare
than anything else on the water.

I spotted her and she wasn't moored so far out that I
couldn't read the name on her creamy bow. She was a
beauty, but she couldn't have been anything else. She had
the jacket and the Stutz to live up to. It could be she also
had Rachel Freeman to live up to. There was no sign of life

on her, but there was nothing you could read out of that. It was still feed-bag time and no action on any of the boats out in the cove.

I had walked down to the jetties where the fishing boats tied up. Inshore from the jetties there's a tangle of weather-grayed shacks. There's no reason to the way they're positioned. Not a one of them sits square to its neighbor but they jut at all angles looking as though a windstorm had picked them up, scrambled them, and then dropped them in this disorderly heap.

Turning in between two of the sheds, I dodged around behind one of them, taking what looked to me like the most improbable turning. I hoped it would seem improbable to Leather Vest. With a little bit of luck I was looking to pick me some daisies. I waited for him and I was waiting in full confidence that he was going to walk into it. He had to be that dumb.

He was. He came charging in. It was all speed and no stealth. It had never even hit him that I could be in there waiting to jump out at him. He had the kind of head that can't hold more than one thought at a time. The one he'd fastened on was that I had dodged in there to lose him and he didn't want to get lost.

Taking him as he came by was easy. Holding him was something else again. I've never wrestled a greased pig, but it's an experience I don't need to have. I had its equivalent with him. I grabbed at his arm, but it slipped through my grasp and I was left with the only thing that was a little less slick. I got a good grip on his leather vest, but it looked as though the vest was the only thing I was going to get. A couple of slick twists and he was out of it, taking off on the run and leaving me with the vest dangling from my hand. For what it was worth I could now see that he was illustrated back and front.

I was amassing a collection of things I didn't need; a button without a coat and now a vest without a button.

He didn't run far, only far enough out of reach to give him a good start on me if I should decide to go after him. There he stopped and worked hard at looking dangerous. He succeeded only in looking miserable, torn between wanting to take off and not wanting to go without his vest.

"Gimme my coat," he said.

"Come and get it."

"You drop it and back off."

"No way. I've never backed off from anything. I wouldn't know how."

"Yeah? Maybe you could be learned."

"If you come and get it, maybe you can learn me."

I was echoing him but I also meant it. I was in the mood for teaching lessons and Daisy Chain had a lot to learn.

"I don't want to hurt you, mister," he said.

I read that to mean it was what he wanted but he doubted that he could.

"That makes us even," I told him. "I don't want to hurt you either. Why don't you just talk me into giving it back to you?"

"I'm not gonna beg."

The way he said it contradicted what he was saying. The tone of his voice was doing the begging for him.

"Don't," I said. "I never give anything to beggars. Begging destroys a man's moral fiber. I don't hold with contributing to that."

"So what do you want?"

"Wrong question or you're the wrong one to be asking it. It's the other way around. What do you want?"

"I want my coat."

"We know that, but a little while back when you still had your coat, what did you want then?"

"Nothing."

"You've been following me for the better part of an hour. For nothing?"

"It's a free country. You can go where you like and I can go where I like."

"And you like going where I go. Why?"

"No reason."

"You can do better than that. Think up a reason."

Damned if he didn't. It was feeble, but he did think one up.

"Your car," he said.

"What about my car?"

"It's a beaut. I like looking at it. I like the way it goes."

"I left it parked. Why aren't you back there looking at it?"

"I was."

"Not for long, you weren't. You came running in here."

"I thought maybe I'd get to talk to you."

"You have and I'm listening. I've been waiting for you to talk."

"I thought maybe you'd let me drive it, just a little, like up the street and back."

"You're a liar and you're not even a good liar."

"No call to be putting names on me."

He tried to sound as though his honor had been impugned and he was about to do something manly in defense of it. I guess he couldn't help its coming out a whimper.

"Try telling me something I can believe."

"Like what?"

"Like who told you to tail me. It wasn't your own idea. You don't have ideas. You're too stupid."

"There you go again. All right, so you won't let me drive your old car. The hell with it. Forget it."

"I forgot it before you ever said it."

I rolled up his leather vest and tucked it under my arm.

Despite my Nebraskan friend's advice, I turned my back on him. When I started to walk away he shouted after me.

"Hey. Where you think you're going with that coat. It's mine."

I turned back to look at him. He had moved forward a few steps but only to match the ones I had taken. He was keeping his cautious distance.

"I'm going back to the hotel with it," I said. "If I don't get back there soon, I'll be too late to get my dinner. Any time you want it, you can have it. All you have to do is come around to the hotel and talk sense. You ask for Mr. Erridge."

I turned again and walked away from him. All the way back to Baby he followed after me shouting the usual curses and the usual insults. If he had come up with anything that was even the least trace original, I'd be passing it on to you, but it was nothing you haven't heard a million times. I don't want to bore you.

I drove back to the hotel. Parking Baby, I did for a moment think of opening her trunk and tossing the vest into it, but the fish sack was already in there. I wasn't reluctant to stink up his vest for him but, if he was working for someone and I felt sure he was, I had this feeling that it might be just as well not to hand out anything on which a brain could make connections.

I carried it up to my room. When I opened the door, the matchstick dropped. Nobody had been in there during my absence or an observant somebody had seen the matchstick and wedged it back into place. I tossed the vest on to a chair and went down to eat, pausing only long enough to wedge the matchstick back in.

I just made it. I was not only the last man into the dining room but, when I got in there, everyone else had already eaten and gone. Except for the waitress I was alone. Dinner was fine. I had forgotten about being hungry but a big bowl of creamy clam chowder reminded me. I followed the chowder with everything else they had going and at midday in those parts everything else is a lot, not that it isn't at breakfast and supper as well. They stoke a man up for the active life and even though I didn't seem to be getting anywhere, nobody could say I was being inactive.

The way it came I could almost have believed it was a proper respect for a man's inalienable right to enjoy his dinner without interruption or disturbance, but I have to call it the way it was. It was an accident of timing.

I had just forked into me the last bite of a hot apple dumpling and I was licking the hard sauce off my chops and washing the whole thing down with a final swallow of coffee when the bird with the boots and the badge came visiting.

"Mr. Erridge," he said.

"That's me."

"I have to talk to you."

"Have a chair, Officer."

He sat.

"Just a couple of questions," he said.

"Any answers I've got," I promised. "But first can I get you some coffee?"

"No thanks. Just ate."

"Your questions? Here or up in my room?"

"Here'll do, Mr. Erridge. Where were you last night?"

"Here at the hotel. I'm staying here."

"But you went out. Where did you go?"

"Up the river. By the rapids. The road turnout where people go to watch the falls reverse."

"Did you see anybody?"

"No."

It was the truth, of course, as far as it went. I had seen nobody. I could have volunteered the rest but I was making some wrong assumptions. Even though I hadn't left my name at the police station, I was thinking that it hadn't made any difference. The way I saw it my visit had been reported and this guy was saving me the trouble of going back to the police station.

A stranger had been in to report an assault. He didn't leave his name but he's the one up at the hotel with the red hair and the blue eyes, not the oil man, the other one.

So I was answering the questions as they came. When he ran out of questions, if there were any left he hadn't asked, I was going to fill him in.

"Did you go there to meet somebody?"

"No."

"At what time did you go there?"

I told him when I left the hotel and when I returned. He took his time about taking that in, looking at me hard all the while.

"We had fog last night. Why did you go to the lookout when there'd be nothing you could see?"

"On an impulse."

"Impulse to do what, Mr. Erridge?"

"To climb down into the gorge. There's always too much wind down in there for any fog to take hold. I had a light and it was interesting to see the tide turn under those conditions."

"You know Sam Ellsworth, Mr. Erridge?"

"We've never met."

"Samuel Coffin Ellsworth?"

"I know the name."

"And you didn't meet him last night?"

"Not to my knowledge."

"What does that mean?"

"It means that if I did, I'm not aware of it. You may have to ask him."

"You have a button, Mr. Erridge."

V

Come on, Erridge. How slow can you be? Day is short for Daisy which is short for Marguerite and there's Leather Vest with daisies tattooed all the way up and down his left arm. This wasn't any courtesy visit saving me the trouble of going back to the police station after dinner. We're off on the wrong foot. We'd better get this thing shuffled around.

"In the fog last night," I said, "somebody made a good try at killing me and he nearly got it made. I went around to the police station and your boy told me to come back after dinner. He could have been more interested, but I did think he'd tell you."

"Likely he will. I haven't been back to the station a couple—three hours."

"Then you don't know anything. I have a button."

I pulled it out of my shirt pocket and handed it over to him. He inspected it carefully.

"This isn't yours?" he asked.

"Not mine. I've been guessing it was Mr. Ellsworth's. I went down to his place this morning to give it to him, but he wasn't there. He seems to be missing. They're worried about him."

"You don't know Sam Ellsworth. What made you think this was his?"

"The button could be anybody's, but the tuft of cloth that ripped off with it is pretty special. There's a picture of Mr. Ellsworth out in the hall here. If this button didn't come off the jacket he's wearing in that picture, then there's more than one guy around here who owns a jacket like that and that's not too likely since it's not any dime-a-dozen kind of jacket. Another thing, I ate breakfast with Jack Humphrey and he'd been telling me that he was supposed to see Mr. Ellsworth last night but Ellsworth never showed.

"How did you get this?"

He was studying the button. I filled him in, gave him the full play-by-play on the fog-wrapped action in the gorge. I could see that he wasn't believing a word of it.

"And you haven't got a mark on you," he said.

"Officer—" I began.

"Bowden," he said. "The name's Bowden."

"If you want to see marks, Officer Bowden, we can take this up to my room. I'll strip for you."

"Someone out of nowhere comes along and hits you in the fog. He ties you up in a sack that stinks of fish and to finish you off he drops you down to the bottom of the gorge where only a miracle can bring you out alive. You don't think he was counting on any miracle. You think he tried to murder you, but you wait till dinnertime till you get around to telling us about it and, when there's nobody around the station to listen, you just wait some more. It's so unimportant?"

It was a good question and on that one I felt I had to lie a little. After all it was a lie that looked to make no difference.

"Call me stupid," I said, "or maybe just stupefied. When I came up out of the gorge, I was beat. I wasn't thinking straight and there was the stink of fish. I was getting sick just on the smell of myself. All I could think of then was getting to where I could skin out of my stunk-up clothes and get under a hot shower."

"You came out from under the shower quite a while back," he reminded me.

"Right, Officer Bowden, right. I was wobbly and feeling weak. I thought maybe breakfast would pull me together."

"Did it?"

"It did but by then I'd heard about Ellsworth not showing up where he was supposed to be last night and I saw the picture in the hall and I thought maybe he and I could have a little talk before I'd go to you."

"What were you going to talk about, Mr. Erridge?"

"I was going ask him why he tried to kill me."

"You thought maybe he had such a good reason you ought to let him do it, or did you think maybe if he paid you enough it could be worth your while to forget it ever happened?"

"If what I had going through my head you want to call thinking, I thought this could be a bucko to whom I owed a poke in the nose. I was thinking I could enjoy hanging one on him."

"That sure you could handle him? On your own story it looks like you didn't do too well last night."

On the surface it was a taunt, but only on the surface. Sitting there eye-to-eye with Officer Bowden, I read it for what it more likely was, a veiled hint of how this fuzz was taking my account of Erridge's encounter in the fog. He wasn't believing a word of it.

"Meeting face-to-face in full daylight, without fog, without darkness, on more favorable terrain, without any sneaking up from behind me, I expected I might do better. A man has to try."

"You have the sack?"

"Locked in my car trunk. It's yours along with the button. I'm not attached to it."

He rose.

"I'll take it," he said.

I led the way out to the Porsche. In passing I called his attention to that fine color photo of Samuel Coffin Ellsworth complete with jacket and buttons. He gave it only a quick glance, didn't so much as break stride to pause and look at it.

"Yup," he said. "I've seen it. I've seen it lots of times."

"It's a great picture of his buttons," I said. "Maybe better of the buttons than it is of him."

Officer Bowden pounced on that.

"Then you do know him," he said.

"Only from the picture, from the little I've heard, from being down to his place this morning where I saw his Bearcat and his shop and the kid he has working for him. Call that knowing him?"

"If you think it isn't a good picture of him, then you know what he looks like. You know him when you see him."

"Only from the picture. If you go back and look at it, you'll see how the buttons come out sharp and clear. His face is a little blurred. He must have moved his head a bit when the shutter snapped."

"You've got all the answers, haven't you?" my inquisitor growled.

"All the unimportant ones," I growled back at him. "Ones like that."

We were out front of the hotel by then and I went straight to the Porsche and unlocked the trunk. Officer Bowden whipped out his notebook and started writing. He was taking down Baby's license number. I fed him her vital statistics and, taking them deadpan, he wrote them down in his notebook. If he caught any sarcasm in my tone, he was taking no notice of it.

By then I had the trunk open. I was leaving it to him to find the sack for himself. It wasn't going to take any Sherlock Holmes. Even Dr. Watson could have followed his nose straight to it. Also it was the only thing I had in the trunk.

He picked it up and looked it over. I have to hand it to

him. Give credit where credit is due. All that jazz. He gave it a close and prolonged inspection. If in the process he got to looking apoplectic, it was understandable. Have you ever tried doing your job while you were being careful not to breathe?

His police car was parked nearby. He stowed the sack in the police car trunk, but the memory lingered on. I was leaving the Porsche's trunk standing open. It needed airing out. I was hoping it wasn't going to need fumigating.

"I have one more item I'd like you to take off my hands," I said.

"Okay. Let's have it."

"It's up in my room."

I started back into the hotel and he came with me. I would have liked to think he was just a sociable type, but I couldn't get it made. It seemed more likely he'd decided I'd be all right without handcuffs. A guy who'd been handled so easily the night before could hardly be a cat capable of giving Officer Bowden any problems, but he wasn't letting me out of his sight.

We trotted upstairs. Before I even had my key in the lock, I saw it. My matchstick had fallen. I left it where it lay on the hall rug but, opening the door, I was more than half prepared for what I was going to find inside the room and that was precisely what I did find.

I found nothing. The leather vest was not on the chair where I'd dropped it. I shot a quick glance at the closet door. That matchstick was still stuck where I'd wedged it. Day had been in to pick up after me, but her passion for neatness hadn't taken the direction of putting the vest on a hanger. She had taken it off my hands instead and I was betting she hadn't shipped it off to the cleaner's.

"Sorry," I said. "I made you climb the stairs for nothing. I thought you'd want to take his vest back to your spy, but it seems like they didn't wait. It's already been returned to him."

If he recognized that I was probing, it didn't bother him any. He made no pretense of not knowing what I was talking about. I'd been followed, but the way he was playing it I had no beef. I was evidently suspect, so what could I have expected?

"Once I'm here," he said, "I'll take a look at those marks you said you have on you."

It bugged me that he wasn't taking my word for them, but I'd made the offer.

I peeled out of my shirt. I was damned if I would go beyond that. I was in no mood for playing show-and-tell with my pants down. He didn't ask for anything more. The collection of abrasions and contusions I had above the belt were more than enough to satisfy anyone. He circled me slowly to do a 360-degree inspection.

At least that was what he seemed to be doing and he had me expecting nothing else. I just stood there, letting him look. When he'd moved around back of me to where I couldn't see him even out of the corner of my eye, I let him go, waiting for him to come around the other side of me.

I'm not saying I was relaxed or at ease or anything like that. I was angry and getting angrier all the time, but I wasn't braced for anything. When he made his move, it took me by surprise.

So when it might have been smart to rip off a little thinking on what might be the meaning and the purpose of it, I did no thinking at all. What I did came as close to being a blind reflex as you can get. It was the simplest sort of action-reaction process. I felt his arm come around my neck and close in with the powered jerk that would tighten it against my throat.

I shot my hands up and took a solid grip on his arm, catching it short of its putting on any pressure. Keeping my hold strong and steady I shot my upper body forward and low, hauling him on to my back as I crouched under him. Before I could even begin to feel the weight of him, I shot upward, straightening my legs.

Just as I came to my moment of full extension I released my grip on his arm. It worked as it had to work. He went sailing in parabolic flight over my head and across the room to hit the floor hard with his ass. He made a soul-satisfying thud when he landed.

I stepped forward to stand over him and it wasn't until he spoke that I even knew I was making fists and holding them cocked.

He looked up at me from where he sat on the floor.

"Assaulting an officer?" he asked.

Half of me thought it was a great idea, but the other half began doing some better thinking. This guy was fuzz and I couldn't make it for it to be any part of his routine to step up behind me and mug me. Assuming, though, against all the likelihoods that this was what he had in mind, it would have to be that he'd been trying something he wasn't much good at.

Your competent mugger comes up behind his victim and whips his arm around the man's throat, bringing it back hard and tight. He does it fast and he does it in one unbroken motion. He's in there and putting the pressure on before you can get your hands up to where they can take a grab on his arm.

Many a man has taken combat training and learned how to handle it the way I'd handled Officer Bowden only to discover that when the real thing comes at him under kill-or-be-killed conditions it doesn't work. He's not been given even that flick of time he needs for getting up there and getting it started. The arm he's supposed to grab isn't grabbable. It's in too tight for him to get his hands around it.

Erridge had brought it off where everything said it

couldn't be done. A cat with some big gift for self-deception might have taken it without asking himself any questions. He would think he had done the impossible, and why not? Wasn't he Superstuff?

I knew better than that. I've been there often enough. I know what hand-to-hand action is like. I don't overestimate myself. Don't take this for any kind of modesty. I can handle myself and, when necessary, I'll give it a try, but I know what the limits are and, more particularly, I know my own limits.

I had to think that Officer Bowden was sitting on my hotel room floor and looking up at me not because Matthew Erridge is so great that he can never be taken but because this same Officer Bowden had been hopelessly slow in the way he'd made his move.

Chew that one over. A man has just made a fool of himself. He's tried something he couldn't handle. He's gotten himself tossed on his ass. He's down there on the floor, defeated and humiliated, except that he's looking up at me with a look that's all cat-in-cream self-satisfaction. His look says he's the winner. He has what he came for.

I made myself hang loose. I put the fists away. I offered Officer Bowden a hand to help him pull up off the floor. He ignored the hand and came up the show-off way, bounding to his feet without using even his own hands to help.

I was impressed and I let him know it.

"You could have taken me if you wanted to," I said, picking up my shirt.

"No point to that," he said.

"And what you did had a point?" I asked.

"Testing," he said.

"And now you know the difference between testing and playing for keeps. Big deal."

Bowden shrugged.

"I thought Eddie was lying," he said. "He most always is.

Sometimes he has a reason for it and sometimes he does it like it's just for keeping his hand in. He couldn't say you didn't take him because you did have the vest off his back. So he had the big story, how you caught him lucky. He tripped on something and he was off-balance when you jumped him. I couldn't waste the time getting the truth out of him. I got it out of you."

He didn't have to spell out any more of it. I had demonstrated to him that I hadn't needed to be lucky to take this Daisy Chain he called Eddie, but that had been a minor consideration if it had ever been any consideration at all. He'd tested to determine whether I could have been taken the way I said I had the night before.

I could match him shrug for shrug.

"Surprise," I said, "is great stuff. There's no way a man can beat the sneak punch. Last night I ran into the sneak punch. This noon I sucked your Eddie into it."

"And after you ran into it last night? What happened then?"

"I've already told you that and I've shown you the marks of it. I've given you the evidence, and that's it, mister. You've got it all. I haven't another damn thing to give you."

"Maybe," he said. "We'll see. Meanwhile what are your plans?"

"No plans. If I get to meet up with Ellsworth, I'll have some questions to ask him. Maybe I'll get some answers."

"What questions?"

"Somebody tried to kill me and I don't know why. He didn't stop to tell me. Mabe it was one of those honest mistakes. He thought I was someone else. Maybe it was because I was where he didn't want me to be, me or anyone else. If so, it was nothing personal. Suppose you were me. Wouldn't you want to know? Just in case it isn't either of those and I've got to watch it doesn't happen again."

"Then you're sticking around? You're not pulling out?"

"Not right off, at least not on my own. Of course, if I'm ridden out on a rail, or isn't that a local custom?"

"We're peaceful around here," Officer Bowden said, "and we're law abiding."

He left it to me to supply the rest. If there was crime and violence it had to have come in from outside. Since that was where I'd come from, it was to be assumed that I'd brought it with me.

"When I'm ready to leave," I told him, "I'll let you know."

"You be sure and do that."

It wasn't the gracious acceptance of a gracious offer. It was an order.

"Do I figure that from here on out I'll be trailing the Daisy Chain?"

"Eddie?" He grinned at me. "If I want you watched, I'll put a man on you who knows how to do it."

He wasn't saying whether he would or he wouldn't. On the whole, he wasn't saying much of anything. I tried with the big question.

"Okay," I said. "I'm a suspect. Do I get to know a suspect of what?"

"You don't know?"

"If I knew, I wouldn't be asking."

"Maybe," he said as he headed for the door.

"No maybe about it."

"Then you'll get to know."

He tossed the words back over his shoulder on his way out. He put the period to them by shutting the door behind him.

Left to myself, I sorted out what little I did know and I tried to add it up. It wasn't nearly enough. I couldn't make it add up to anything.

Leaving the room, I didn't bother with the matchstick. It wasn't going to tell me anything I didn't already know. Day with her maid's set of room keys came and went. She had been in to do up the room while I was under the shower and she had seen the button. I could read that part of it easily enough.

At that time she had attached no importance to the button. Assuming it was mine, she'd gone to the closet, looking for the jacket that would be missing it. She had taken my jackets out and put them back, having found nothing that needed the leather button. Maybe it would have been part of her supermaid routine to sew it back on for me just as she took it on herself to send my stuff out for cleaning and laundering.

Finding nothing that needed her needle, she had dropped the button into the ash tray. Sometime later something came up that gave her new ideas about the button. She knew I hadn't left it in the room because she'd been in there while I was down at breakfast. You remember. She had gone back to do up the bathroom.

What could have come up to change her thinking on the button I could only guess at. She'd probably heard that Ellsworth was missing and, working at the hotel, she would know the photo gallery. That at least. Being a local, it was likely that she had even more direct acquaintance with Samuel Coffin Ellsworth and the snazzy jacket.

So Eddie wouldn't have been Officer Bowden's man. He wouldn't have been any kind of fuzz. It would have been Day who put him on my tail. Exploring after a chance at blackmail? Could be.

The perfect hotel maid who wouldn't lightly go to the police to turn a guest in? That perhaps, but also the good citizen who couldn't with a clear conscience hold info back from the police even when it was info about a good tipper.

To that extent I could work it out. She'd have Eddie tail me. Either way she might do that, working up more leverage for a blackmail bid or helping herself to resolve her conflict between her loyalty to a hotel guest and her duty as a citizen.

But then Eddie was a bust. He picked up nothing and he lost his vest. Handling Eddie as I had, I knew I wasn't making myself a tattooed friend, but I had no way of knowing that in the process I was making myself an enemy back at the home pad. He wanted his vest back and that was no problem.

Day got that for him, but whichever way she'd been planning on working it, I'd changed her mind for her. I wasn't going to be anybody's easy patsy for a touch of blackmail or, on the other line of thinking, I'd been unkind to her faithful and devoted Eddie. The armful of daisies had to be a mark of devotion. It had to be read for a more ardent declaration than any common garden variety pair of entwined hearts. It had been more than enough to make her go out gladly to do Erridge dirt. That would teach him not to rough up her property.

Just out of my head I could take it that far, but I was still left with the big question. There was the turning point, the information or the incident that came up and that to Day's way of thinking made that leather button lose its innocence.

Officer Bowden had said that I'd get to know. I wasn't in the mood to wait for it. There was nothing in my hotel room that was going to tell me. I went back downstairs. A breeze off the water was caressing the Porsche and it had blown Baby's trunk clean. I shut it and went back into the hotel. I was looking for a local I could talk to or, more exactly, one who would talk to me.

There was Day, of course, and in the past we had talked, but any good feeling I'd developed in that quarter had to be down the drain. There was the waitress, but she had served me my dinner and, even though we had been alone together in the dining room, she had tipped me to nothing. Either she'd had nothing to give me or she'd been no more inclined to be informative than had been Officer Bowden.

I was left with Andy. On my experience of him, Andy wasn't bright. He was never going to be anybody's pet conversationalist. Andy was the hotel bartender. It was a full-time job, but the way he carried out his duties was at least half-assed. The first time I hit him for a drink I could see right off that his skills behind the bar went only as far as pulling the tab off a can of coke. Anything past that was way past Andy.

The other customers growled at him. Jack Humphrey did and I could guess that the locals always had. I undertook to educate him. I showed him the right way to draw a brew. After no more than looking at the feeble mix he put before me when I asked for a dry martini, I commandeered the ingredients and put one together for myself. He watched and since then day-by-day he was learning. Day-by-day we had also been building a rapport.

I sauntered into the hotel's little bar. It was the hour when any bartender who takes his vocation seriously is taking advantage of the lull to polish glasses, make up a batch of bar syrup, and replenish his stock of lemon twists.

Andy was not so engaged. Maybe he didn't even know that he should have been, and doing his job right was certainly out of character for the guy. What he was doing, however, hit me as even more out of character. He was reading. If anyone had asked me, I would have said Andy couldn't read without moving his lips and I would have been right about that. He was moving his lips.

What made it crazy, though, was the thing he was reading. It wasn't a comic book and it wasn't one of the paperback jobs they abstract from a hit movie and put out for the cats who weren't up to digging it the first time around.

It was a fifteen-pounder and fancy, a coffee-table book if I ever saw one. They hit the bookstores every December and move on to the cut-rates in January. *Treasures of the Louvre. Crossbows and Arquebuses. Brass Rubbings of Olde England.* That kind of a book.

I didn't get to see which one it was because on my entrance Andy flipped it shut and hurried it out of sight behind the bar. He looked like the kid who, when teacher turns his way, slips his Nick Carter into the geography book.

"Double martini?"

That was Andy's stab at reading my mind. You can see that his mind reading was on a par with his bartending. Who goes for double martinis within an hour after lunch even where lunch is called dinner?

"Bourbon," I said.

He reached for the Virginia Gentleman. That was one of the things I'd taught him. He didn't pour me the bar bourbon. Sloshing the whiskey into the glass he let it rise to a level that made a double look so small you'd think it hadn't yet come out of diapers.

I looked at it.

"That's no drink," I said. "When there's that much of it, it's a footbath."

"On the house," Andy said. "You need it."

"Mad at the boss?" I asked. "Working him up a bankruptcy?"

"Taking care of a friend," Andy answered. "Celebrating."

"And what's to celebrate?"

"Joe didn't take you in?"

"Who's Joe?"

"Joe Bowden."

"What would he take me in for?"

"Murder."

"Murder? Who's dead?"

"Sam Ellsworth. First off they weren't sure because they pulled the body out of the rapids, and the water and the rocks they'd stripped him naked and his face was so mashed up knocking against the rocks you'd never know it was a face."

"And now they're sure?"

"Yeah. They got Doc Hill to take a look."

"Who's Doc Hill?"

"Dentist. He knows his work and he knows the work he put in Sam's mouth."

Andy was more than a mine of information. He was an oil well. He gushed the news.

VI

It had been about midmorning when the body had been spotted hung up on a rock at the head of the rapids. I knew where that would be, about a quarter of a mile upriver from the place where I'd run afoul of Ellsworth's leather button. That far upriver the road had no guardrail since there it was above the gorge. There was just an embankment that sloped up steeply from the road level and then down again gently to the river's edge.

"It figured to be an accident," Andy said. "Guy on a motorcycle misses the road turning and he's going fast enough on his motorcycle so he mounts the bank and the bike bucks him off into the rapids. Tide coming up the rapids does the rest of it and nobody sees him till it's ebb and what's left of him shows up stranded on the rocks."

"They found the motorcycle?" I asked.

"Some pieces of it down the rapids."

Listening to Andy, I was working on it for myself, matching up times. Midmorning would have been when I was on my way down to Ellsworth's place or just about arriving there. On Andy's estimate it had been about a half hour after the body had first been spotted that Doc Hill had been summoned for a look at the fangs. Andy put it at about another half hour before the word got around that the body had been identified. It was the remains of Samuel Coffin Ellsworth.

I wondered how quickly they had gotten the word down to Rachel Freeman. Even if they had called her the minute they knew, even the half hour would have put me back on the road. By the time I'd made it all the way back, the word, of course, had reached the hotel and Day had set her boy up to watch for me and tail me. All the rest followed.

"I guess I know why Joe didn't take you in," Andy said.

"That's easy," I told him. "He had no reason to."

"Some cops would have done it but Joe, he's careful. Joe wants a lot of reason and he'll wait till he's got it. But then, look out! I was you, brother, I'd take off."

"He told me to stick around. I said I wouldn't pull out without telling him first."

"Yeah. And he knows your car and he's got your license number."

Andy sighed. I couldn't tell whether the sigh came out of the agony of thought or out of pity for Erridge's plight.

"That doesn't matter," I said. "There's no reason for me to run."

Andy didn't agree. He'd thought up a stack of reasons and he lined them out for me.

"You were in a fight last night and you came up with a button off of Sam's coat," he reminded me.

"Bowden knows all that."

"By tomorrow he's going to know more."

"There isn't anything more that could have anything to do with me," I argued.

"He's got Sam's body over to the hospital," Andy explained. "They're doing an autopsy. When they find that Sam was dead before he went into the river and it was only his dead body the tide was knocking around on the rocks and they find what it was that killed him, Joe'll have everything he wants. You can figure you have till then."

It was full of iffy spots and Andy was disregarding them. If they found that Ellsworth was dead before he went into the river. If they found indications that he'd died by murder. Thinking about those ifs, I quickly got to where I was agreeing with Andy. They could be disregarded. On what I knew they would have to be.

My earlier line of thinking, that it had been Ellsworth who came up behind me in the fog and clipped me and that, while he was stuffing my head in the bag, his button had ripped off and landed in the bag with me, just wasn't holding up under the weight of all this new information. To assume he'd done all that and then tooled off up the road to have his motorcycle accident and do himself in would be plain crazy. After all, I did know that the motorcycle hadn't gone into the river up there at the head of the rapids. It had hurtled past me while I'd been pulling myself together down in the gorge.

The fact that pieces of it had turned up strewn the length of the rapids didn't mean a thing. That wild rush of incoming tide had battered it against the rocks. In a matter of minutes the water would have broken it up and washed its pieces along to strand them here and there.

It was a good bet that Ellsworth had gone the way I did, except that he'd carried all the way. The force of the tide had taken him just as it had taken the motorcycle, carrying him up through that four-hundred-odd-yard stretch of rapids, battering him against the rocks, stripping the clothes off him, and beating his body to an unrecognizable pulp.

I was in trouble. Andy was right about that, but the way I was seeing it, I couldn't have run even if I had wanted to. In any case, I didn't want to.

Meanwhile Andy was working up a plan. For the Porsche the run up to Calais and the border crossing into Canada would be only a matter of minutes. He wasn't recommending that. Baby was too conspicuous and, even though she could easily outrun the fastest wheels Bowden had at his disposal, even Baby couldn't outrun a phone call. I'd be slamming into a roadblock at the border if not before it.

"I know where I can get a panel truck," Andy said. "I

park it here out back and you slip into it and stay there out of sight. I won't go Calais way because if Joe got the word to them up there, they could be looking inside of everything. I'll take you the long way, up back country to the woods and up through the woods. I can get you all the way up to the St. Croix. You can make it across."

You have to know that stretch of country. The U.S.-Canadian border along there is the St. Croix River and back from the ocean front it's great tracts of woodland. The woods are paper-company property but they are open to hikers, picnickers, campers, and canoers. In season they're open to fishermen and hunters. You can drive through them for hours and never meet a soul, and any good swimmer who's not afraid of cold water should be able to swim the river.

It's done all the time. For some years now those woods along the St. Croix have been family-reunion country. A guy who chose Canada instead of Vietnam sets it up with his folks. They take themselves a camping vacation up in those woods near the river. There's nobody else for miles around. He rows across or swims across and they get to be together for a while. The family, of course, could go across legally and visit with him where he's living in Canada, but there are some who would never trust it. Anywhere they go, anybody they see looks like CIA or FBI to them. They use the woods.

It could be done and it was a cinch that Officer Bowden knew it. It could even have been that it was one of the things he was waiting for, that as much as the results of the autopsy. If Erridge was suspect, Erridge on the lam would be more than suspect.

I didn't feel like going into any too-proud-to-run routine with Andy. I kept it practical.

"I stay and I co-operate," I said. "I can do that because I

know I didn't tangle with Ellsworth. If I bug out, I just pin it on myself."

Andy grinned.

"So what?" he said. "You're out of the country. You're safe."

He was overstating it, but it was about what I might have expected of him. I had him tagged for being that stupid. Also it was just the way the stupid cats are likely to act. They whip themselves up what they think is a clever scheme and they get carried away with it. Here was a chance for that dope, Andy, to pull off something smart. He wasn't going to let go of it easily.

"Safe?" I said. "Not safe enough. The way the Canadians feel about draft evaders or even about deserters is one thing. The way they're going to feel about a fugitive who's been charged with murder is something else again. There's a thing they call extradition."

"You don't wait for that," Andy argued. "You fly right down to Costa Rica. That's one place. There's others."

"Not for me," I told him. "Thanks anyhow."

I slipped off the bar stool and started to move out of there.

"Think about it," Andy urged. "Tonight. Right after I shut down here, that'll be the best time. I can get a canoe and put it in the truck. I'll take you across and paddle back. It'll be easy."

"Don't bother. I appreciate it and all that, but I'm not going."

"Think about it," Andy repeated. "You have till tonight. It's got to be tonight. After that it'll be too late."

There was no good in going on with that. I hauled out of there and, if I did any thinking about it, it wasn't the kind of thinking Andy had urged on me. I was touched by his offer. I told myself it wasn't his fault that he was stupid. He had offered to help. He had given me the feeling that his offer did not come out of his holding any belief in my innocence. The lug seemed to be thinking he was helping a killer. I could have resented that, but I didn't resent it. It was something, after all, that the guy should want to get me away no matter what I might be or what I might have done. If he liked me that well, it is pleasant to be liked.

I wondered about that. It was a big thing for him to be wanting to do on nothing more than our aquaintance across the bar. It seemed much too big a thing. Andy, however, was a fidgety type, the kind that gets bored and unhappy with small-town life and itches to get away to the big cities because he thinks it's there that the action is.

That could also be a factor. For him it could be getting a piece of the action, for once being a part of something that was widely apart from the local humdrum. I also thought of another possible factor. Could it be that it wasn't his liking Erridge so much as it might be a dislike he might have had for Samuel Coffin Ellsworth.

I wandered along the hall and took another look at the photo of Ellsworth in triumph. It could have been my imagination, but the man in the picture did look every inch the snotty bastard. He looked like a man who could have had enemies. Even as I was thinking it, though, I was telling myself that this was thinking after the fact. The man had been murdered.

If other people were waiting for autopsy results before making up their minds about that, Erridge didn't have to wait. I knew. So a cat who gets himself knocked off is all too likely to have been a cat who had enemies or at least one enemy.

Heading for the outdoors, I got as far as the lobby. There I ran into Henry Haskin. The old boy was at the postcard rack giving studious attention to one of the cards. It's one you'll see on sale all over the state, one of those cute fakes they put out for the tourists. A shot of a big Maine potato is superimposed on a shot of a railroad flatcar so it looks like a spud so big it takes the whole of a flatcar to carry it. I guess it got to the farmer in my Nebraska friend. I could imagine that the way he was looking at that potato would have been the way he looked at greasy Eddie's overdecorated pelt.

He spotted me and said hello. I said it right back at him.

"I thought you'd be on the road," I said.

They had been on the road a long time and were ready for settling in somewhere for a couple of days before going on with their travels. They had decided on this hotel for their stopover. Mom was upstairs doing a little unpacking.

"We thought maybe we'd like to see all them tattooed crazies you told us about," he explained. "And then there's this other thing. I don't believe it, but we're going to see for ourselves."

"What other thing?"

"After you left back there where we were having our picnic, mom and me, a lot of folks came along. Police they were and other folks. We got talking to a man and he said that, when the tide comes in, those falls there turn themselves around and the water doesn't go down like natural. It goes up. This we've got to see. I don't believe it."

"You'll see it," I told him. "It's the big deal around here."

"That one, he was following you? You got rid of him?"

"He wasn't anything," I said. "We had a talk. He's off my back."

"That's good," Haskin said. "I didn't like the look of him, an ugly customer if I ever saw one."

"Not nearly as tough as he tries to look."

The old man was worried and the words I'd thought would be a relief to him only seemed to get him to worrying the more.

"I hope you're not thinking as how I had ought to be minding my own business," he said, "but I'm old enough to be your father, at least your father. I've got grandsons, they're grown and married and with families. I've done a lot of living. I've had the time for it and I've seen a lot of life. You've got to watch the mean ones and it's the mean ones who aren't tough enough to do anything with their fists that you've got to watch the closest. They're the kind'll put a knife in a man's back or they'll come up behind him and shoot him in the back. You don't mind my telling you?"

"I don't mind," I said. "I'll remember it."

"I don't want to go mixing in your business," he persisted. "But if there's anything I can do to help. Just give a yell. Hank Haskin'll come a-running."

I grinned at him.

"Thanks," I said. "I'll remember that, too."

I left him with the superspud and I went out to Baby. So far as I could see, there was nobody keeping watch. The hotel was down a tree-lined street off the main drag and there was never heavy traffic to roll past it. Now under the afternoon sun the street seemed to be empty. The whirr of a lawnmower said that somebody was around and a snick-snick that had to be hedge clippers indicated somebody else, but neither of them showed.

I mounted the Porsche and we pulled away. I held her down to a walk. If Bowden was having me watched, I wasn't about to do anything that would make his man nervous. Haskin had said something interesting. Putting it together with something I'd had from Andy, I came down with an itch to see a thing or two for myself.

Loitering out the river road, I was still some distance short of the turnout that looked down on the rapids when I began seeing signs of what Haskin had mentioned. Cars were parked at the roadside in an unbroken line. There were evidently so many people up ahead that the cars had overflowed the turnout parking.

I drifted on by and they were there, police cars, officers,

and just folks. Among them there was a good sprinkling of
the Leather Vests. I looked for Eddie Daisy Chain but he
wasn't in evidence. I had a hunch he was off in hiding while
he stuck some blowout patches on his machismo.

I didn't stop. I couldn't have if I had wanted to. There
was no place to sit Baby down unless I went to the end of
the line of cars parked along the road. I went on to the end
of it and stopped there. It was a little beyond where I'd
wanted to be, but I walked back.

I climbed off the road for it, going along inside the line of
parked cars to walk on the grass of the embankment. I was
well above the rapids. I was looking for the place where the
body had been hauled out of the river.

Even though I was sure that I knew where it had gone in,
I wanted to see for myself what the fuzz had been looking
at before I'd tipped Bowden to where he might better look.
The embankment was as I had remembered it. It rose
steeply off the road but it was nowhere much more than a
yard high and on the other side it sloped down to the river
in a gentle and even incline.

A motorcycle traveling at high speed in the fog and stray-
ing from the road could easily have carried over the rise and
rolled on down into the river but never without having left
some trail of its passing. It would have done more than
flatten the grass. It would have churned up the dirt and dug
itself conspicuous ruts.

I walked the full length of the embankment down past
the head of the rapids, all the way to the place where the
cliff reared up and the gorge began. From that point on
there was the guardrail, so I knew that I had covered the
place where the body had hung up on the rocks. Nowhere
was there the first sign of torn up grass or churned up earth.
The picture as I'd had it was standing up.

When I reached the beginning of the guardrail, I ran out
of walking room. I edged between two of the parked cars

and came out on the road. Turning back I headed for the place where I'd left Baby parked. There didn't seem to be any point in going on down the road to the turnout. I'd been ahead of the police in covering that ground.

But even from where I was I could see that Baby was not alone. The Porsche had picked up some company while I was walking. A police car was double-parked beside her and a cop was looking her over. As I drew nearer, I recognized him. It was the kid who had been holding down the police station during the dinner hour.

He saw me and decided against playing with the Porsche's horn. He came away from Baby, jumped into his fuzz buggy, rolled it just far enough past Baby to give himself room for a tight U-turn, swung it around, and came roaring back to bear down on me. The way he handled it, I could see he was proud enough of his driving to want to do some showing off. It wasn't good enough to call for that much pride. I could picture him cutting a notch in the handle of his revolver for every fender he dented.

Pulling up alongside me, he made it a brake-screaming, circus stop.

"Erridge," he barked.

I didn't like the bark. Bowden was going to have to take an hour some time to teach his boy manners.

"Mr. Erridge," I said.

He ignored the correction.

"The chief wants you."

I walked on toward the Porsche. He went into reverse and moved along beside me.

"You heard me."

The bark was taking on a sharper edge, maybe even carrying the promise of a bite.

"I heard you. I'm getting my car. Then you can lead the way. I'll follow."

"Nothing doing."

I stopped.

"Cool it, hard boy," I said. "Your chief wants me. Okay. It's nice to be wanted. What do we do now?"

He opened the door of his police car.

"Get in and don't try anything funny."

I got in and slammed the door after me.

"Right," I growled. "No time for comedy."

Once he had me in the car, he eased along, none of the dash he'd been showing just before. He was having his moment of being top dog and he was getting too much fun out of it not to prolong it.

"It's a good thing for you that you didn't try to take off," he said.

"When I came into the station house, did I look as though I was about to take off?"

"You was reporting an assault. You didn't say you tangled with Sam Ellsworth."

"I don't know that I did," I told him. "It's my guess that I didn't."

"Oh yeah?"

"You forgot something."

He had been crawling along but now he almost came to a stop. He was looking himself over, taking inventory of himself. Maybe he thought I was taking a tactful way of telling him his fly was open. It wasn't.

He glared at me.

"What?" he asked.

"You're supposed to read me my rights," I told him. "You have to do that first thing or do you want the Supreme Court to rap your knuckles?"

"You think you're smart."

I'd taken some of the fun out of it for him. He gave the fuzz buggy a decent flow of gas. We moved.

"That," I said, "is something I hadn't thought about. I think you're stupid."

He was normally red-faced. The red slid along the spectrum in the purple direction.

He pulled into the turnout and flicked off his ignition. There was parking room for him, evidently the place he'd pulled out of to go after me. I reached for the door handle. He made a move toward slapping my hand away, but he thought better of it. Leaving his hand poised in midair, he reverted to barking.

"Stay where you are."

Never taking his eyes off me, he backed out of the car and came around in front of it, watching me through the windshield. He came all the way around to my door and wrenched it open.

"Oh, service," I said.

"Get out."

He wasn't giving me any extra room, only barely as much as I needed. He was making a big show of keeping me hemmed in, giving me no chance at making a dash for freedom. Taking more room than he was giving me, I came into a landing on his foot. That backed him off. I knew I wasn't making myself a friend, but he annoyed me and I wasn't half ready to accept the thought that I might be in a spot where I'd need friends.

Bowden came around from in back of the car and took over.

"I'd like you to do me a favor, Mr. Erridge," he said.

"Anything I can do, Chief."

My escort looked as though he would have liked to fade out, but he was pocketed against the guardrail. He had no fading room. Bowden drew back to let me pass and we walked away from Hard Boy.

"Can't you do any better than that?" I asked. "Or is Meathead a whiz with traffic tickets?"

"He's a whiz with the likes of your friend, Eddie," Bowden said. "It's not often I need him for anything else. He's got a strong back. A boy gets too drunk to walk, he can carry him."

"Good enough," I said. "Now what's the favor?"

"Since you're here," Bowden said, "would you mind going through what you did last night? Just run it through for me."

"Last night it wasn't a solo."

"I know," Bowden said. "It takes two to tango."

He got that one off as though he had just fresh thought it up. I didn't wince. I've got great self control.

"If I can leave a lot of it to your imagination," I said. "Getting clipped, getting stuffed into the fish sack, getting banged against the rocks when I was pitched down off the ledge, I can show you where I was when each happened. If that'll do?"

It was all he'd had in mind and he did appreciate my co-operation. I caught myself beginning to like the guy, but I put myself through a quick attitude correction. The harsh and tough detective and the kind and gentle detective and between them they use the suspect like a tennis ball, bouncing him back and forth between them till he collapses over the net and is ready to babble.

I went through the motions for him and that meant going through them for a large and interested audience. I kept it as bare as I could, no re-enactments. If my audience felt that my performance lacked punch, that was the way I wanted it. If the Leather Vests and the rest of the locals went away bored, that was all right with me. Of course, they didn't go away. Erridge was the only show in town.

I climbed the guardrail and Bowden followed after me. I led him around the blackberry thicket and showed him the place where I'd bumped into the motorcycle.

"Want me to climb down the way I did last night?" I asked.

He did want it. I repeated the climb. He watched me go

and, when I stopped, he climbed down and joined me at the lower level.

"This is as far as I came on my own," I told him. "The next thing I knew I was on the bottom ledge with the tide beginning to reach for me."

With his eye Bowden measured the drop I'd indicated.

"All that way?" he asked. "There are a couple of ledges in between. What about those?"

"I don't know. I must have hit them on the way down and bounced off them or rolled off them. I look like it and I feel like it."

"Uhhuh. How far down had you planned on going or were you going to watch from here?"

"It wasn't any good watching from here," I told him. "This far up it was all fog. I was going to climb on down till I'd be under the fog. I had it figured that about halfway down would do it."

"Okay. Mind going on down?"

"If you mean the way I did it last night, I do mind."

Bowden grinned.

"On your own power," he said.

I did the rest of the descent, all the way to the bottom ledge. When I stopped there, he again came down and joined me.

"Here?" he asked.

"Here."

"You're sure. Incoming tide, even when it's not a big one, floods this. You'd have been swept off."

"You're telling me. I only just made it up out of here before I was swept off. The water was grabbing at me when I got myself pulled up here."

I indicated the next ledge up.

"The tide sweeps that one too," Bowden told me.

"It wasn't running heavy last night but anyhow I didn't

hang on waiting for it. I went on up as soon as I'd worked the sack up off my head."

"The motorcycle crashed down past you. Where were you when that happened?"

"Just above here, this next ledge up. I was standing there. I'd just gotten myself clear of the sack. That's how I could see it when it came tumbling past me."

"Close?"

"Any closer and it would have conked me, probably would have knocked me down into the rapids."

"You think that was the idea? You think it was aimed at you?"

"It couldn't have been. The fog was hanging so close above me that I could stick my arm up and lose my hand in it and from there on up it was solid all the way to where it lay on the road. From up above nobody could have seen me to aim anything."

"Then how do you explain it?"

"I don't explain it, Chief. I'm waiting for you to come up with the explanation."

"It's your story, Mr. Erridge," Bowden said. "You want me to believe it."

"I've told you what happened. Now, Chief, if you find it hard to believe, I can't say I blame you. I find it hard to believe myself, but since it happened to me, I have no choice. I've got to believe it. I've given you all the facts. Do you want theories?"

"You have any?"

"Somebody was here. What he was doing here I have no way of knowing. Maybe he was here to kill Ellsworth. That's one possibility. Or maybe he was here for something else and Ellsworth was like me. He came barging in on the cat when the cat couldn't have anyone barging in on him. Either way he was cleaning things up after whatever it was he'd been doing here. Maybe it was after murdering Ellsworth. Maybe it was after he'd been doing something else and murdering Ellsworth was part of the cleaning up process. Certainly what he tried to do to me was part of it and getting rid of the motorcycle was more of the same. It's the only way I've been able to figure it."

"It takes a lot of believing, Mr. Erridge."

"Okay," I said. "Let's try the other possibility. Matt Erridge, who never knew this Ellsworth character, had never seen him and had never even heard of him, ups and murders the guy. Matt Erridge who, on his record, has never had anything against motorcycles, dumps a perfectly good motorcycle into the rapids. He's had a good night's hunting. He's made a kill, but that isn't enough for him. He has to have a trophy to take home with him. Ellsworth was no moose, so there won't be antlers. He wasn't a fox, so there's no tail. But Erridge has to have something. He takes a button. That'll do it. He takes it home and he'll have it stuffed and he'll hang it over the mantelpiece. How much believing is that going to take, Chief?"

"You're an engineer," Bowden said.

It was neither a statement nor a question. It was an accusation. I could make nothing of it but that Bowden had been doing some homework on me.

"Looks like you don't know much about engineering, Chief. It isn't done with buttons."

Bowden ignored that. He went on past it.

"You're an engineer," he repeated. "You're working on something you're going to want to develop around here. Sam Ellsworth was a conservationist. Whatever you've been looking into, he was going to block it. He was in your way."

"And the gang I work for gave me a contract on him," I said, piling on the sarcasm. "I rub Ellsworth out but I need to have proof to take back to show that I carried out my orders. The button was going to be my proof. Oh, come on, Chief!"

"I've been thinking about the button, Mr. Erridge," Bowden said. "I don't make so much of that. Sam Ellsworth was no easy man to take. He had a lot of muscle on him and he kept himself in shape. He used to be a wrestler. When he was in college, he was heavyweight champ. Wrestled all over the country and everybody he went to the mat with, Ellsworth pinned him."

I was getting tired of this.

"You were talking about the button," I said. "Now all of a sudden it's going to be pins?"

"He gave you a battle and he didn't do too bad. You showed me the marks he put on you. You came out the winner, but you'd been in a battle. He'd gotten enough licks in on you to knock you dizzy. You weren't thinking straight and it just never entered your head that Day would be doing your room while you were under the shower. You were too dizzy to think about the button. Otherwise you'd have thrown it away. It didn't have to be any problem. It would have been easier than Ellsworth and easier than the motorcycle."

"And when I got over being so dizzy, why didn't I get rid of the button then?"

"It was too late. Day had seen it and you knew she had seen it. And this isn't theory, Mr. Erridge. It's what you told me yourself. You came back to the hotel and you had to have your shower and your breakfast before you could begin thinking straight. You said that yourself."

VII

If there had been a good audience for our climb down into the gorge, the crowd had just about doubled when we came back up to the road. The time for the afternoon turning of the tide was approaching and, whenever that happened at a convenient hour, it drew a throng of watchers. That much I'd discovered on my first day in the area. If I wanted to explore it without everybody and his brother there to watch me, I had to do it with a light at a nighttime turning. For daylight exploration, I had to catch it on those days when it came so soon after daybreak that for tourists it was still sleepytime.

The increased crowd therefore was inevitable. We'd had the fuzz watchers and none of those had pulled out. Now they had been joined by the tide watchers. The Haskins were there and that was to have been expected. It was a large part of what the old parties had stopped over to see. Under the circumstances they were getting their money's worth. They had also wanted to see more of the Leather Vests. They had a great assortment of those among the fuzz watchers.

Mom and Pa caught my eye and both of them started doing all sorts of vague things with their hands and faces. You know what it's like when someone's trying to throw you signals and at the same time trying to act as though they're not even looking at you. They think they're doing something that'll be only for you. It's not going to mean anything to anybody else. It usually comes out that it doesn't mean anything to you either. They just look as though they'd come down with a sudden case of the twitches.

But they weren't the only people I recognized among the new arrivals. There was someone else and the sight of her brightened Erridge's day. It was the little Peachcake out of Ellsworth's shop, Rachel Freeman. It was a cinch that she wasn't there to see the water come falling up. Even if she wasn't a native who'd been seeing it all her life, she had certainly been living in that part of the world long enough for the novelty to have worn off.

I couldn't classify her among the idle fuzz watchers either. I hardly knew the kid, but even on the very slight acquaintance I had with her, I was certain she wasn't the type. It wasn't that I'd tabbed her for a softie. She just seemed too cheerful a sort and too healthy to come up with any taste for the morbid.

When I'd seen her earlier, she'd been worried. Now she looked sick. If she had come to watch, it wouldn't have been for the fun of the thing. On the way up out of the gorge Bowden had told me I could take off, but only within the limits he had laid down earlier. I was to stay within reach. I'd be hearing from him.

So once I was back over the guardrail I headed for Rachel. I needed to know a lot more than I did about the late Sam Ellsworth, stuff like who he could have tangled with since it hadn't been Erridge, and Rachel Freeman seemed the best possible source for that kind of information. That she was also the most delightful potential source I'd met up with could also have been a consideration. A man should have some pleasure in his life and I was pushing myself through a day that had been all too short on enjoyment.

I grinned at her and I waved at her. She made a try at an answering grin but she couldn't get it made. She did wave back at me. She knew I was coming to talk to her and she was waiting for me, but it wasn't to be that easy.

Working my way through the crowd, I was waylaid. Mom and Pa grabbed at my arms and hung on.

"You're in trouble," Mom Haskin said.

She could have been telling me that I'd torn my pants or I needed to wash my face. She didn't approve of trouble and she wanted me out of it.

"We've been looking at them crazies," Pa said. "Other parts we've been in we've seen motorcycle gangs and anywhere they are, they mean trouble. One of them can be bad enough but when it's a gang of them like here . . ."

"It's all right," I told them. "They leave me alone and I leave them alone."

"That one before, he wasn't leaving you alone."

I wanted to shake loose as quick as I could. All the time I was tied up with the old folks I was keeping my eye on Rachel. She could be getting tired of waiting. I didn't want her to go away.

"He was a one-man deal," I said. "No gang stuff."

"That don't say he won't bring his gang into it, whatever it is," the old man insisted.

"They always do," his wife added. "They're like wolves. They do everything in packs."

I couldn't make it to believe that between baking cookies and putting up the jams and jellies, this dear old party could have sandwiched in much experience of either wolves or gangs, but I wasn't up to telling her she didn't know what she was talking about.

"You hadn't ought to be going around alone the way you do," Pa warned. "You need somebody with you, somebody to watch your back."

"The police are taking care of that," I said. "Nothing to worry about."

It could even have been true, but anyhow it was the right thing to say. For the moment it relaxed them and they let me go.

"All the same you take care now," Mom told me.

"If you need us, we'll be around," Pa added.

"Yes, indeed," said Mom.

I didn't know what to say. I managed as best I could. I kissed her on the cheek and I shook his hand. He had a grip you could have expected from a man maybe forty years younger and not often then. As I turned away from them to go over to Rachel, he sent me on my way with a friendly whack on the shoulder. That shoulder, of course, had been tenderized by slamming against I don't know how many rocks but, even if it had been in perfect shape, that whack would have registered. The old boy had a hand that couldn't have weighed much less than a sledge hammer and it was no softer.

I rallied from it and pushed on to Rachel. She was still waiting.

"Hello," she said. "I've been looking for you."

"Hello," I responded, "and that's the nicest thing that's happened to me all day."

"Oh, for God's sake. Don't be gallant."

"Now that's a silly thing to say. I can't help it. It just comes naturally. What if I were to say to you, 'For God's sake, don't be beautiful'?"

"Men," she muttered. "Men can never understand that there are women who don't go for nonsense or even that there are times and circumstances when nobody can go for it."

"And this is one of those times and these are some of those circumstances?"

"For me," she said. "I don't know about you. Maybe you're so used to people being murdered even when it's done so horribly that there's nothing left of him that anyone could recognize, nothing but his teeth."

She wanted to cry and scream and she wasn't letting herself do it. She was holding it all inside her, but it was there and she was taking a beating.

"I know what you need," I said. "You need to come away from this. We'll go some place where there aren't all these people. You can put your head on my shoulder and have a good cry. You're not going to be right until you've had it. Crying inside is no good. You'll come down with a case of tear-poisoning."

"I have cried. I cried on Sarah's shoulder."

"No good," I said. "You picked the wrong shoulder."

She stamped her foot.

"Oh, come off it, please."

I came off it.

"You were looking for me," I said. "What made you think of looking out here?"

"I didn't, Mr. Erridge."

"I like it better when a beautiful girl calls me Matt."

"There you go again," she groaned.

She started walking but not as though she was walking away from me. I fell in beside her, figuring she couldn't object to that since she was going my way, up the road to where I'd left Baby parked.

"Sorry, Rachel," I said. "I'll watch it."

"I asked for you at the hotel, but you weren't there and your car wasn't there and Andy—" She broke off. "You know Andy?" she asked. "He's the idiot they have tending bar."

"I know Andy. I know the idiot."

"What is he, Matt? Your keeper or what? He kept telling me I didn't want to find you. I was to go home and keep out of this whole thing. It was man stuff and nothing for a girl to get herself mixed up in, but above all I was to keep away from you."

"He is an idiot. I thought he was my friend."

"He seems to think he has to protect you from me. He didn't say it in so many words, but he came close."

"But you didn't listen to him. Good girl."

"I didn't know where to go to look for you except for thinking that with everybody else coming out here, you might have come, too. Anyhow if you hadn't, I could have talked to Joe Bowden."

"You thought he'd know where you could find me?"

"I thought he ought to know about your coming to see Sam this morning," she murmured. She was finding it hard to say. "You see," she hurried on to explain, "it just didn't occur to me that you were a detective. You don't think of detectives driving Porsches, but you are, Matt, aren't you?"

"A cat who drives a Porsche? I am."

"No, you know what I mean. A detective?"

"No."

"You act like one."

"How do they act? I guess I've been doing the wrong things."

"Coming around looking for Sam this morning of all mornings. Climbing down the rocks with Joe Bowden and explaining things to him down there."

"I'm not a detective, Rachel. I'm a suspect."

"That's a horrid joke. It's not a bit funny."

"I'm in a horrid predicament and I can't remember when I last laughed."

"Who suspects you?"

"Chief Bowden, the chambermaid at the hotel, and Andy even though Andy keeps it politely covered up. That's just to name a few. I don't know who all else."

"That's ridiculous. Joe Bowden is in over his head. He's never had a murder before. I was in high school with Day Ruisseau. When they passed the brains around, she was some place else. She wasn't there even when they were passing out the simple horse sense. As for Andy, he's worse. At least Day's a demon cleaner. Andy's nothing."

"And me, Rachel?"

"Sam would have liked you, Matt. I think you would have liked him."

"How about you?" I asked. "Have you always like the people Ellsworth liked?"

"You're about to be silly again." She changed the subject. "You were asking me how I knew where to go to find you," she said. "I drove out this way and I didn't see you anywhere on the road and I didn't see Joe Bowden either. I couldn't park at the turnout, so I drove on till I found a place I could park and I saw your car. I parked beyond it and walked back thinking you had to be back there in the crowd and I'd missed seeing you. Of course, you were down in the gorge with Joe."

I did something then that was the last thing I wanted to do. It happens to me from time to time. Something rears up and stops me from doing what I'd like to do. The flattering word for it is integrity. Stupidity describes it better.

"So then you thought I was a detective," I said. "What I can't dig is what you thought I was before that. A good guy because you wanted to come and talk to me? A suspect because you thought you ought to tell the chief about me?"

She hadn't thought about what I was. I was just a man who'd come around looking for Sam Ellsworth. I was a stranger. It could have been that I'd been passing through and, not having found Ellsworth, would be moving on. She'd been thinking that I might know something and it could be something important without my realizing that it mattered at all.

She'd been thinking that if I moved on, in Baby I could move fast and far and I'd never even hear about Sam Ellsworth and how he died. She'd been thinking it was important for me to know about it just in case I could help.

"And now that I do know about it and I'm not a detective but a suspect," I said, "shouldn't you be talking to Bowden instead of to me?"

"What makes you a suspect?" she asked.

There was no reason for not telling her. Evidently Andy hadn't but somebody would. I wanted her to hear it from me.

"Somebody tried to kill me last night," I said. "The way I read the evidence, I happened to get in his way after he'd killed Ellsworth and was cleaning up after himself. The way those others are reading it, I was in a fight with Ellsworth and killed him and I'm trying to sell this other story."

We had come to the cars. We stopped by the Porsche. There was a Volks just beyond it that had to be hers.

"Someone tried to kill you?" she gasped. "Who?"

"I don't know. It was dark and in the fog. He came up behind me. I never saw him."

"But you thought he'd killed Sam? What made you think that?"

"I didn't think it then. Back then I didn't even know that Ellsworth existed. It was just that someone jumped me and only narrowly missed killing me. I thought it might have been Ellsworth. When I barged in on you this morning, I was looking for him to ask if and why."

"But you didn't know Sam existed."

I was confusing her.

"Let's go somewhere to sit and talk," I suggested. "How about the hotel bar? Since you refuse to cry, you do need a drink. I'll buy."

She looked at Baby and she looked at the Volks.

"I can't go off and leave that thing sitting on the road," she said.

"Drive my heap," I said. "I'll follow in yours."

"You can't mean that."

I put my hand out.

"Keys," I said, "or don't you want to trust me?"

"Me trust you?"

She looked from the Porsche to the Volks and she even laughed.

So that was the way we went back to the hotel with her driving Baby and me following along in the Volks. If, when I tried at the first to give you some idea of how beautiful this kid was, I didn't get it made, this time around, I should be doing it. I let her climb into Baby and take the wheel and I wasn't even beside her to police it. If I'd been around back in Trojan Helen's time I don't think I would have let Helen do it. I wouldn't have let her drive my chariot.

To be going around with anything as great as this Rachel and to be doing it in separate cars had to be something like being married and in separate rooms. A man can't help coming down with a bad case of the wants, but apart from that I wasn't sorry.

Along with everything else there was to like about Rachel Freeman there was the way she was with wheels. She did nothing to Baby that I wouldn't have done and after no more than that short ride back to the hotel she was a new girl. She was glowing.

"Lovely, lovely, lovely," she burbled as we did the return swap on the car keys.

"Like my car?" I asked.

"Love it."

"And me?"

I was expecting more of the same. She was going to tell me to come off it, but she said nothing. She just rose up on her toes and kissed my cheek. It was a let's-be-friends kiss or maybe even an I'll-be-a-sister-to-you kiss, but don't great oaks from little acorns grow? I had my little acorn. I've always been an optimistic type.

I took her into the bar. Don't imagine that I didn't think that my room upstairs would have been more private, but with the Rachel Freemans it's better not to push too hard. I comforted myself with the thought that the room could seem more private than it was. Marguerite Ruisseau had keys. Let's not forget that.

In the bar there was nobody but Andy, Andy and that coffee-table-type book he was studying. Again he was quick, maybe even frantic, to hurry it out of sight and the look he gave us was anything but welcoming. I didn't know whether it was annoyance at being caught in the act of pretending he was literate or anger at Rachel for ignoring his advice. He'd told her to keep away from me and now she comes walking in on him to flaunt me in his face.

"What do you drink?" I asked her.

"Ginger ale," she said.

"Come on. You need something more medicinal than that."

"The only thing I like Andy doesn't know how to make."

"Andy doesn't know how to make anything except what I've taught him. I'll make it and Andy can learn."

Andy muttered something. It was inaudible, but, reading his lips, I dug it to be something unsuitable for a lady's ears. Doesn't that make it unsuitable for your eyes?

"A brandy Alexander," she said.

"You've got to be kidding."

"I know. Just the thought of it makes men gag, so it had better be the ginger ale."

"Brandy Alexanders," I told her, "are fattening."

"Not when you can practically never get one," she said.

"Okay," I said. "As long as you're going into it with your eyes open."

"And my tongue hanging out," she added.

I started to go around back of the bar. I'd been there before when I gave Andy his martini lessons, but now he wasn't having me. He liked none of this and he was all for letting us know it.

"Do it around on the customers' side," he snarled. "I'll hand you the stuff. What does it take?"

"Cognac, crème de cacao, heavy cream."

He dug the brandy and liqueur off the shelves and slapped them on the bar in front of me.

"Ain't got no cream," he said.

"The kitchen'll have it," I suggested.

"This ain't the kitchen. It's the bar."

"And the kitchen is only a couple of steps away. You can make it there and back without working up the first drop of sweat."

"I can't leave the bar."

"Since when?"

"Since always. The boss don't like it."

"All of a sudden?"

"I done it too often. He's getting mad."

I didn't know about the boss but I did know about me. This was a new Andy, as stupid as ever but now obnoxious to boot. I didn't make fists. I know I didn't because I was being supercareful not to, but there's that little tensing of the shoulders a man will show when he's thinking about wanting to push somebody's face in and he's not letting himself do it. I guess Rachel caught that.

She dropped a lovely little hand on my arm and she laughed.

"Oh fiddle," she said. "I know my way to the kitchen. I'll get it."

I knew the way, too, and I could have gone, but I had this feeling that I didn't want to leave her alone with Andy, not even for a minute or two. The stupid twerp was bent on being ugly and she didn't need anybody giving her a hard time. Anyhow she was gone before I could make the first move.

"What's eating on you, stupid?" I asked the dope.

"It's you that's stupid," he said. "Joe catches you with her and that'll be it. He'll lock you up and then there won't be one damn thing I can do for you."

"There isn't one damn thing I'm going to let you do for me," I told him. "So forget it and start behaving yourself."

"You're so big on giving advice," Andy said. "How's to give yourself some and how's to take it? She works in Sam Ellsworth's shop. After what happened to Sam, Joe's not about to let anything happen to her."

Run that over in your head, Charlie, and see how it plays for idiocy. Erridge is a mad dog. He'll just as soon kill you as look at you. Any girl who values her life should be shunning him. So let's load him in a van and take him up to the St. Croix where we can paddle him across to run ravening among the Canadians.

I could have told him that it had been right under Chief Bowden's inquisitive snoot I had joined up with Rachel Freeman. I could have tried to straighten him around on what he did as a substitute for thinking, but just then Rachel came back with the cream. Does a man waste himself on an Andy when he can be making time with a Rachel? This man doesn't, not ever.

I left him to his nonsense and did the big show-off job with the cocktail shaker. No measuring. The whole thing done with Erridge's unerring eye and steady hand. One part crème de cacao. One part cream. Two parts cognac. Ice and the virtuoso shaking job that could have won me a job in the rhythm section of any band.

Andy came up with the Virginia Gentleman bottle, but I took it away from him and poured my own. I was carrying the memory of the one he'd poured me a while back and I wasn't in the market for another of those dimensions. I was drinking with Rachel. I didn't need to be anaesthetized. I didn't even need to be stimulated. Rachel was heady stuff.

We took our drinks to a table as far removed from Andy as we could manage. It wasn't much in the way of removal. The hotel bar was small, not nearly big enough for swinging a cat; but this was a staid hotel and a staid neck of the woods. Swinging cats swung elsewhere.

Rachel sipped her gop and looked blissful, but the bliss didn't quite erase her worry. Booze doesn't have much chance to get at you when you take it wrapped up in all that cream.

"You were going to tell me about you and Sam and why anybody would think you'd want to kill him," she reminded me.

I fed her the whole package, the button, the sack, the motorcycle, and Chief Bowden's ideas on motive.

Hearing that I was an engineer and looking things over with a project in mind, she sidetracked for a bit. I'd pretty much expected it. Her boss had been big on ecology. She wasn't likely to be relaxed about it.

"Would it mess up the gorge or the cove or anything?" she asked.

"Only temporarily, during the installation. Once we'd have it in, you wouldn't know it was there except for having smaller electric bills."

"And the salmon? Will it drive them away again? They've only just come back."

"With my high regard for sex? You think I'd let anything stand in the way of a spawning salmon?"

"No, seriously, Matt."

"Seriously, Rachel. I'm up here to see if it can be done without lousing up the landscape, without polluting anything, without disturbing the salmon or annoying the lobsters. Can we do it without disturbing the oysters and clams in their beds? Those are the questions I have to answer and, unless I can answer every last one of them affirmatively, my people aren't going to be interested. They're not looking for a fight."

"Have you explained all that to Joe?"

"He hasn't asked me."

"But you should tell him. Joe's not stupid. He's inexperienced but he isn't stupid. If he's going to think that sort of nonsense, he should be suspecting that oil man. He's the one Sam was fighting."

"Jack Humphrey? Forget it. He wasn't in the gorge last night and I was. He hasn't come up with a nice set of lumps to show he'd been in a fight and I have. He wasn't caught in possession of a button off Ellsworth's coat."

"I don't see any lumps."

She was looking at me and I almost had reason to hope she was liking what she saw.

"Under my shirt and under my britches. Come up to my room. I'll strip for you. They're something to see."

"Not necessary," she said. "I believe you."

I sighed.

"So chalk up another time Matt Erridge has been done in by his honest face."

"The oil man," she said, dragging me back on course, "what do you know about what he's got under his shirt and britches? Has he stripped for you?"

"I never thought to show any interest. He's an all-right Joe, but he's the wrong sex."

"Can't you forget sex even for a minute?"

"Since you ask, I can't and I dread the day when maybe I will."

"Rise above it."

"I don't like it up there."

"Matt, stop being a fool. You're in trouble."

"Nothing like the trouble I'd be in without sex. But back to Jack Humphrey. You can't be serious about him?"

"I'm not," she said. "I'm not because the whole idea is crazy. It's just that if Joe Bowden is going to be having these stupid ideas, the Humphrey man would make it a little less stupid."

"How?"

She lined it out for me and it was as she said, logical enough in its limited way but still stupid. Humphrey and Ellsworth had been about to meet head on. They were going to be fighting tooth and nail. Between them there was real enmity.

Then there was Erridge. He was getting ready to come into it with a proposition that would be just what Ellsworth would have needed to finish off any last hope Humphrey could have had of bringing off his deep port and oil refinery deal.

"It would be this way," she said. "The Humphrey man thinks you and Sam are getting together and he knows that once that happens, he's cooked. He kills Sam to stop his meeting you and he tries to kill you to stop what you're doing."

"I get killed," I told her, "my people send up another man. I'm not the only engineer there is. Maybe the best but not the only one."

"With you gone and Sam gone he'd win himself some time. Maybe he can get his scheme through before another man can come up here, before anyone around here knows there's a more attractive alternative to what his company wants to do to the cove."

"Hey, baby," I said. "Stop. You're beginning to convince yourself."

She patted my hand.

"Relax," she said. "I'm not convincing myself, not beyond thinking with Joe Bowden's mind. It makes no sense because I don't think the Humphrey man could be a fool."

"He isn't," I told her. "But what are you thinking when you get out of Bowden's head and back into your own?"

She told me and she was no fool either. Some of it I already knew, but she provided the more detailed picture. Jack Humphrey was up against massive opposition. I'd known that. It seems to me I told you as much, that he had nobody on his side but the Leather Vests. The big boys, the movers and shakers, were all solidly against him.

"Sam was the most vocal of them all," she explained, "but he didn't pull any great weight. If anything is to be done or not done along this stretch of the coast, it was never Sam who had the control. Actually there's only the one man who matters and that's Knees Coffin."

"E. E. Coffin?" I asked.

She nodded. "It's Edward Ebenezer," she said. "In the family everybody calls him Knees."

"And you're family?"

"Not really. Do the geneology thing all the way back and everybody around here is related to everybody else, but Sam was family. His mother was a Coffin. He and Knees were cousins. If Sam pulled any weight around here at all, it was only through that, being a cousin. It's Knees who gets listened to in Augusta and, for that matter, in Washington as well."

"You know him?"

"Yes."

"How does he stack up as a drinking man?"

"Knees?"

"Knees and his crowd."

"Knees likes his Medford rum. A small glass before dinner, a small glass before supper, a small nightcap."

"And on parties?"

"He doesn't party."

"He partied last night."

I gave her a rundown on the Humphrey hangover, and found that she knew all about it. Ellsworth had told her. They were going to take turns drinking with Humphrey till they had him loose-tongued enough for him to hand them the stuff they'd need for defeating him with his own words.

"Knees does things like that," she said. "It wasn't the first time."

"Ellsworth was expected. Everyone else showed. He didn't get there."

"I know. Knees called me last night. He thought I might know where Sam was. He was furious. A Knees invitation is a command performance."

Suddenly it came to me that maybe I was coming around to thinking with Chief Bowden's head. A stoned Jack Humphrey takes off from the Knees Coffin binge and runs into Ellsworth. He gets the idea that Ellsworth hadn't shown at the party because he was off working something up with Erridge.

That could have made him plenty mad, but in his right mind he would certainly have known he could do himself no good killing either or both of us. In his right mind, but had he been in his right mind? Knees Coffin and his cohorts could pass the drinking around, but Humphrey had been in there alone. He couldn't pass anything around. It had been the plan to get him stoned and, if there was one thing clear, it was this. What Edward Ebenezer Coffin planned, Edward Ebenezer Coffin accomplished.

VIII

It made sense up to a point, but only up to a point. I got back into my own head and, as soon as I'd given even the first thought to the rest of it, it fell apart.

"There was that sack that stank of fish," I said, thinking aloud. "Not fresh fish, dead fish that had been around too long."

"When the men go out after crabs," she explained, "they dump them in that kind of sack. Used day after day, the sacks can get to be more than repulsive."

"This one was. It was a lot more than. Wouldn't it have to be someone local? Where would Jack Humphrey or I, for that matter, come by such a much-used sack?"

"So much used," she said, "that it had been thrown away. Anybody could have picked it up somewhere along the shore or even off the dump."

"You'd rather not think it was a local boy?" I asked.

"I don't like thinking it was anybody, but it was somebody, wasn't it? Sam was killed. You were almost killed."

"It was somebody," I said. "Now here's another thing and it's better than the sack. Ellsworth was due at E. E. Coffin's party last night and he never got there. He didn't make it because he was otherwise occupied. He was busy getting knocked off."

"That's it," she said. "Joe Bowden may be thinking Sam was busy with you, but we know it wasn't you."

"I know it," I said.

She was having none of that.

"We know it," she insisted.

"How? Because I have blue eyes?"

"Because you have too much integrity."

"Does it show?"

She smiled.

"Of course, it shows," she said. "You'd like to wean me away from brandy Alexanders but, when you make me one, you make it so much more delicious than any I'd ever had that you have me more than ever addicted. That's integrity."

"Could you use another?"

She could.

I went over to the bar and worked on it. Andy hadn't returned to his book. Reading was obviously only for his solitary times and, until I'd seen him at it, I would have guessed he didn't read even then.

"And Ellsworth wasn't busy with Jack Humphrey either," I said while I was assembling her glop. "We know that because Humphrey did get to the Coffin party, or did he?"

"He did. When Knees called me, he said Humphrey was there and everyone else was there, everybody but Sam and what was keeping him."

"So that's it." I went back to the table, bringing her the calories. "What was he doing? Where? With whom?"

"There's only one thing I can think of," she said.

"Think it," I urged, "and out loud."

"We're peaceful around here," she said. "The nearest we come to violent crime might be a Saturday night drunken fight. I remember once Joe arrested a wife beater. That was an event. People talked about it for years."

I saw no place that could take us.

"Drunken fight," I said. "I don't think so. The guy who worked on me wasn't drunk. He was too much in control for a drunk and he took me at close quarters. I would have smelled liquor."

"Past the rotten fish?" she asked.

"I didn't smell that until afterward. That was when I came to and he was nowhere near me. I'm thinking of before, when he came close enough to chop me down. I smelled nothing then and I'd have noticed it if he had a breath."

"Vodka?"

"Leaves you breathless? That's a myth. It's less noticeable than gin or rum or whiskey, but when there's been enough of it to make a man drunk, at close quarters it's noticeable."

"Then maybe it was what I've been thinking," she said.

"Like what?"

"Burglary," she said. "Breaking and entering. There's been too much of that and Sam was worked up about it. Nobody liked it but for Sam it's been a special worry."

"He's been losing stuff?" I asked.

"No. It isn't that."

"If anything was broken or entered last night, wouldn't the word be around by now?"

"It might be," she said. "It might not, but it didn't have to be last night."

She explained. It never happened in a house where people were in residence. Folks go out for an evening or even over a weekend and they come home to find they've had burglars —it was never like that. It was always houses that were locked up and that were going to stay that way for some considerable time.

"Summer people," she said. "They're here three or four months of the year. Otherwise they may come up for Thanksgiving and again for Christmas, usually for a week in the spring to get the garden started and then someone tends it for them till they come up in the summer. It could also be some of the year-round people, the older ones. They're retired and they go some place warmer for a couple of mid-winter months."

"Hit their places soon after they leave," I said, picking up on it. "Then it's months before anybody knows there's been a burglary and by then the trail is hopelessly cold."

"Especially the way the antiques market is today," she said. "Things move so fast and most of it is unidentifiable. It's only the occasional thing that anyone could recognize. It was different when only something rare and wonderful brought a good price. Now it's Victorian things that used to be a dime a dozen and even Art Deco."

She told me how it went. The way I dug it, it had been skin off Sam Ellsworth's ass. He was in the business.

"Sam never bought anything that had been stolen from any of the local houses," she explained. "None of it was ever offered to him. The thieves are smarter than that. They take it south, out of the immediate neighborhood. It goes to dealers in Augusta or Bar Harbor or Rockport, maybe even down to Portland or Boston."

"They're less careful down there?" I asked.

"They have no way of knowing. That was a big part of what had Sam so exercised. If someone he didn't know turned up with something they wanted him to buy, he always had the nasty thought that it might be something stolen out of a Rockport or Bar Harbor summer place."

"He was doing something about it?" I asked.

"Anything he could. A couple of times he just took losses. One of the summer people would come up and find a horsehair sofa gone. They'd come to us looking for a replacement and they'd see a sofa that was just like the one they lost. We knew it wasn't their sofa. Sam knew where he bought it and when. He'd had it in stock before they'd locked up at the end of the previous season. It was another one so much like theirs that there was no telling the difference, certainly so for most of these people. They're a bit vague about the details of things they own. One had carved rosebuds and another has carved rosebuds. They never notice the difference in the angle of a carved rosebud."

I caught it.

"And rather than let people go away suspicious," I said, "he gave them the thing and just took the loss."

She nodded.

"It hasn't happened often," she said, "but even the few times it put us in a position where there was no winning. Let them have it and Sam could never be certain that they weren't still thinking he had bought stolen goods and had to make good because they'd caught him at it. Tell them it wasn't theirs and they'd think he was a thief. People buy something in an antique shop and, even if it's something that's most common, they convince themselves that they own something unique. His best hope was that they'd think he'd bought the stolen thing in ignorance and good faith and he was so honest that all anybody had to do was tell him it was stolen goods and he made good immediately. It's a nasty position."

"You said he was doing anything he could. Anything besides taking these losses?"

"Nothing really, but he was trying. He'd get to suspecting someone and he'd try to watch him, but it all seemed rather futile. He was no detective."

"And last night he saw someone and watched him," I said, "and he was a good enough detective to get it made. The catch is he wasn't good enough to do it without the thief detecting him."

She moaned.

"You didn't know Sam," she said. "I can just see him. I can hear him. He was always so sure he could handle anything. I can see how he would do it. He wouldn't find out what he wanted to know and just quietly go away and tell Joe Bowden what he'd learned. He'd confront the man and denounce him and expect the man to come along docilely to be turned over to Joe."

"I've seen his picture. He looked like a man who kept himself in good condition. I would have said he could handle himself in a fight."

She looked at me.

"And I would say you could handle yourself in any situation," she said. "You took the surprise blow and you went down."

"I wasn't confronting anybody. I wasn't denouncing."

"For Sam any blow thrown at him would have been a surprise blow. He was an Ellsworth and his mother was a Coffin. You'd have to know what that means around here. When an Ellsworth frowns, he expects people to cringe. When a Coffin speaks, he expects people to crawl."

"Okay," I said. "So who?"

"Sam caught him with something Sam knew was stolen." She was thinking aloud. "He got rid of Sam. I suppose he got rid of the thing as well, whatever it was."

"Maybe not," I said. "Maybe with Ellsworth rubbed out, he'd think he could keep it and sell it. Nobody else to know."

"Fingerprints maybe?" she said.

"The gorge," I said. "The gorge doesn't have to mean anything. It's a place to get rid of a body and make it look like an accident, but I have a hunch that was only part of it."

"What else?"

I was only beginning to shape it up in my own mind, but I gave it to her as it came. Ellsworth had set out for E. E. Coffin's Humphrey workout fairly early in the evening. It was almost morning when his motorcycle was dumped down into the gorge. That was a lot of hours in between. How had those hours been filled?

"He was following his man all that time and didn't catch up with the incriminating stuff he needed until shortly before I turned up," I said. "That's most unlikely. The way I make it, he saw something on his way to Coffin's place and he had it all pinned down pretty quick, and pretty quick he was dead."

She picked it up from me.

"That's it," she said. "It was the wrong time for disposing of Sam's body. That had to wait till just before the turn of the tide. You came along not just after he'd killed Sam but just after he'd disposed of the body and when he was on his way up out of the gorge to dispose of the motorcycle."

"Right. But what was he doing down in the gorge?"

"You've been down there," she said. "You know what it's like. There are big rock fissures and shallow caves, a couple of big ones and a lot of little ones. He could hide the body in one of the big ones and nobody looking down from above could ever see it and even someone climbing down would be likely to miss it. Also who would be climbing down there on a foggy night?"

I shook my head.

"Yes and no," I told her. "He killed Ellsworth early in the evening and he hid the body in a fissure or a cave down in the gorge until he could pitch it down into the rapids and have enough water to batter it against the rocks. That much holds up."

"Then what doesn't?"

"Taking the body down into the gorge to hide it. I know that climb. Nobody could make it carrying the body of a big, heavy man."

She shuddered.

"It's awful, but did he have to carry the body? He lifted the motorcycle over the guardrail and hid it behind the blackberry thicket. He could lift the body over the guardrail, couldn't he?"

"Yes, but there he's stopped. He had to leave the motorcy-cle up there at the top. He couldn't carry that down and hide it in one of the caves. That's it. He couldn't carry the body down either."

"Drop it off the top to the ledge below," she suggested. "Climb down there and drop it to the next ledge, and so on. Why not that way?"

I studied on it.

"Possible," I conceded, but only just possible. "It would be a long time to mess around with it if it was early evening and before the fog set in. Also it would be too much out of control. The body could roll. It could hang up some place where he couldn't get at it and then, come daylight, it would be there for everyone to see, a murdered man. He wanted it to look like an accident."

"Then how?" she asked.

"Ellsworth followed him and caught him with something and there's only the one place Ellsworth could have caught him and that's down in the gorge. He followed the man down there and down there the man turned on him and killed him. The killer hid the body, went up to the road and hid the motorcycle and then came back just before the turn of the tide to dispose of the body and the motorcycle. Then I came barging in."

She thought for a moment.

"Yes," she said. "Yes, but it still won't work out. It would have to mean that he had whatever he'd stolen down there and that's impossible. It's too wet. Even above the highest tide mark it's always dripping with water down there. It would be hopeless for old furniture."

"It couldn't be furniture," I told her. "Even a small piece, lighter than a man's body and lighter than a motorcycle, but still impossible for carrying down through that climb."

"Glass or china? Could you carry it down and up without smashing it? It's no good, Matt."

"Hold it. Not so fast. What about silver?"

She jumped.

"Matt," she gasped. "The Revere bowl."

"One if by land and two if by sea?"

"Yes. Paul Revere. He was a silversmith and a great one. Even without all the bicentennial build-up Revere pieces have always brought a fortune. Right now there'd be no limit."

"And one of Paul's products has been ripped off?"

"Nobody knows for certain, but maybe. It's the craziest story. There's this lovely old man, has a beautiful shop down in Ogunquit. He's a specialist in old silver. The poor man has cataracts and he's been as good as blind with them. They've been developing slowly and he's been waiting the longest time for them to reach the stage where they'd be operable. He's in Boston now. He had the operation just this past week, but last Sunday he was in his shop. He always has an assistant with him but the assistant had gone off to get him something."

"And blind and alone he had a visitor who wanted to sell him a Revere bowl?"

"A bowl anyhow. He knows silver like nobody else and he's been so long hardly seeing at all that he's reached the place where he can all but see with his hands. He took the bowl and ran his finger over it, feeling for the mark. He found it, and just on touch he couldn't be sure it was the Revere mark but, of course, he wouldn't have been going ahead on no more than that anyhow. He'd want someone to look at it who could really see it."

"Reading a hallmark by Braille," I said. "That would be something."

"A blind man with a lifetime of training might be able to do it," Rachel said, "but he, for all his sensitive hands and knowledge of silver, just couldn't. On just the feel of it, he knew it had to be either the real thing or a good reproduction. He was inclined to think a good reproduction. If it was Revere, he'd want to know where it came from. When you are dealing at that level, provenance is important."

"Also the danger of buying stolen stuff," I added.

"He wanted to wait for his assistant to come back. The man who was trying to sell it was impatient and nervous. The old man could feel that the man was getting jumpy and suddenly the man snatched the bowl out of the dealer's hands and ran out of the place."

"And that's no way an honest salesman behaves," I said.

"Exactly. There's a dealer's association and the word went out. All the dealers were alerted."

"And somebody up around here did have a Revere bowl ripped off?" I asked.

"Not that we know of."

That seemed peculiar.

"Wouldn't you know? A thing like that?"

"Summer people," she said. "They keep to themselves. Of course, it's largely our fault. We keep to ourselves."

"People lock up a house and go away for months. Do they leave something that valuable? Wouldn't they take it away with them or put it in storage?"

"Or lend it to a museum," she said. "You'd think they would, but the very rich ones, you never know. Certainly if it was a reproduction, they wouldn't bother."

"And nobody sees the inside of their houses, just themselves and burglars?" I asked.

"Other summer people. House guests. They're always having house guests from all over the world. Some of them are jet set."

"Servants?"

"Not local. They bring them with them when they come or send them up ahead to get the house ready. It's ridiculous but it takes years before it breaks down and then only if there are children."

She explained that. Summer family kids did play with

local kids. Then the kids grow up, summer and local, and that generation takes over. Since they knew each other as kids, they go on knowing each other. At that point, even though they are still summer people, they get to belong just as though they were locals, but it has to develop that way, in the second generation.

As you may remember, I'd been the last one in the dining room for dinner and I'd been running a well-filled afternoon even before the happy ending set in with my meeting up with Rachel. After that we'd been a good long time kicking it around in the bar. So we were still in there when it came to be suppertime.

We had only just worked the thing out between us when the bar began filling up. Jack Humphrey came in and Mom and Pa Haskin. There were also some transients, just checked in for the night. Humphrey gave me the nod but he went off to be by himself. From the way he looked, he could still have been in the hair-of-the-dog stage and when a man's drinking dog hair, he doesn't want to do it convivially. He's done enough of that to last him for a while.

Mom Haskin zeroed in on what was left of Rachel's Alexander and, as soon as I'd finished introducing Rachel to them, we had to give the old dear an explanation of the glop.

Now that was a drink she thought she could enjoy. Result: Erridge was enlisted to throw one together for her and, while he was doing it, Rachel went out to phone. She was going to call Joe Bowden and put him on the right track.

She came back disappointed. I could read it in her face.

"He doesn't go for it," I said.

"He's not in his office and he's not at home. Nobody knows where he is and it's no good trying to explain anything to the dimwits he has on the force. I just left a message. He'll come here as soon as he gets in."

"You'll want to be here," I said. "Have supper with me. We can eat while we're waiting for him."

"I said we'd be in the bar."

That was easily taken care of. I just passed the word to Andy. When the chief turned up, Andy was to tell him he'd find us in the dining room.

"He knows the way," I said. "He found me there this noon."

We took our time over supper but it wasn't as tête-à-tête as I could have hoped. After a few minutes Mom came in and a little later Pa followed and they established themselves at the table next to us. After that it was tête-à-tête-à-tête-à-tête. We were a cozy foursome.

We finished supper and we loitered over coffee waiting for Bowden to turn up and make it a quintet, but he didn't show. It was my guess that he wouldn't get Rachel's message until after he'd had his supper or that, even if he did have it before, he would leave acting on it till after his meal. In that country up there they take eating time seriously.

If I could have been somewhere alone with Rachel, I would never have noticed the passage of time. I was with Rachel, of course, but far from alone. With all that Haskin dilution in the mixture, the waiting around seemed to be stretching out to multiples of forever. I got restless.

We went back to the bar on the chance that Bowden had turned up and might be waiting for us there. Mom Haskin excused herself. She'd had a big day and she was going up to their room and lie down. Pa, it seemed to me, took the idea with more happiness than solicitude. He urged her on her way. It was easy to see that the Alexander was catching up with her. It's a slow acting tipple. Wrapped up in cream, the alcohol does no lightning job of filtering through the stomach wall, but it does filter through and the blood picks it up and carries it to the brain or some such.

Mom took off and Rachel hit the phone again. No dice.

Bowden had still not returned to either his office or his home. He hadn't yet received her message.

"I'm going back out to the gorge," I said. "I've got a good idea of where to look."

Rachel was all for coming along. I looked at her feet.

"In case you haven't noticed," I told her, "you're not the little old lady in tennis shoes. Those aren't the shoes for rock climbing."

"I can stay at the top and watch you search," she argued.

"What about Bowden? You said you'd be waiting for him here."

She wasn't happy about it.

"We could leave word for him, tell him where we've gone."

I'd hoped she wouldn't think of that, but the last thing I'd have wanted to do was to tell her why. If I was to run into anything, I was prepared to handle it, but I'd be in better shape for it if I didn't have to worry about protecting her.

"He's got to be sold," I said. "He'll be in a better mood for listening if he doesn't feel we've been running him around all over the place."

It was feeble, but it was the best I could think up.

"You don't want me."

She was beginning to sulk and mostly I don't like sulking females; but on her even that looked good.

"That'll be the day," I said, "but it's no good getting the chief mad."

She surrendered. When I left the bar, she was climbing up on a bar stool. Maybe Andy was better company than none. Pa Haskin came upstairs with me. It was beginning to be dark and it was likely to be full dark before I'd be through poking into caves and fissures. More than that, however, even in the dusk I was going to need my light if I was going to see into the holes in the rock face.

I assumed Haskin was going up to join his wife, but at the

top of the stairs he didn't go along to their room. He followed me toward mine. Thinking that he'd gotten turned around on his room location, I told him he was going wrong.

"I'm going with you, young fella," he said. "You need somebody behind you to watch your back."

If he wanted to, I could see nothing against it. I didn't need to worry about having to take care of him. This was a spry old party. For all his age he was still heavy-muscled and from the way he moved you could tell that he hadn't even begun to creak.

You know the second law of thermodynamics, Charlie? Everything slows down. Everything wears out. Pa Haskin was the old cat who had it beat. The second law had not yet caught up with him.

I trotted down the hall to my room and he trotted along at my heels. I fished out my room key, unlocked the door and opened it. The room was dark. Day had been in and she had pulled the shades against the afternoon sun. That was part of her regular routine. Now that the sun was gone and with nothing but twilight the other side of the shades, the room was like night.

I reached for the light switch. If the light came on, I never saw it. I remember hearing the swishing sound close in behind me and that's all. Erridge flopped into his own private blackness, which made it twice inside twenty-four hours and that's like picking up a habit. I have habits and some of them may be bad ones, but this now, getting suckered into unconsciousness? This I didn't need.

IX

How long I was out I had no way of knowing. It seemed like no time at all, but when I'd come out of it far enough to take stock of myself, I knew it had been longer than that. The room wasn't as dark as it had seemed when I first opened the door on it, but that meant nothing.

You know how it is. You move out of the light into the dark and it takes a moment or two before your light-accustomed eyes adjust to where you can see in the dark. I hadn't had that moment or two.

Regaining consciousness, however, was different. That was going from dark to not quite so dark and, vague as they were, I could make out shapes and locations. I was in my room, on my bed. I seemed to be alone and the door out to the hall had been shut.

I had a mouth full of gag and the gag had been firmly tied in place. My hands were tied behind my back and my feet were bound together. I was tied at both the ankles and the knees. I tried to strain against the bonds, but I couldn't break anything and I couldn't work up any give. It was a good, tight job even though it was a humane one. There were no cords biting into my flesh and there was relatively little circulation cut-off.

Some broad bands of stuff had been used for tying me up. It was my guess that it had been done with my neckties. I caught myself wondering whether, when they weave that silk poplin Atkinson makes up into the ties he sells in his Dame Street shop in Dublin, the Irish mean to weave the stuff strong enough for this kind of use. I put the thought away for consideration at some more suitable time. I had more pressing matters for the skull to work on.

It didn't have to be that I'd been out any great span of time. More than a moment or two, enough more for picking me up off the floor and putting me on the bed, for gagging me and tying me hand and foot. I worked at remembering what had preceded my blackout.

I remembered the swishing noise and I remembered Pa Haskin. By flexing my neck and pressing my head hard against the mattress in every position I could manage I explored for some area of tenderness. I had come up with such an area at the back of my neck the night before and from it I'd known where I'd been clipped.

I found that same area now and there was still some tenderness in it but less than there had been earlier. It was obvious that it hadn't had any freshening up from a second blow. So this time I hadn't been chopped. It hadn't been a rabbit punch. There had been that swish of something whipping through the air. There was only one guess I could make. This time it had been a sap, soft and heavy, designed to produce maximum unconsciousness with minimum contusion.

But saps don't jump up out of nowhere and swing themselves. There has to be a hand to wield one and hadn't Pa Haskin been right behind me, watching my back? Pa Haskin? They hadn't arrived till noon. They were touring all over the place and hadn't even been in the neighborhood the night before. Or hadn't they? I had only their word for what their movements had been.

All over the place ripping off locked-up houses? Picnicking in that turnout, keeping an eye on their hidy-hole down below? Waiting till dark to go down into the gorge and bring up whatever they had hidden down there, the Revere bowl or whatever it was? When the area filled up with fuzz

and fuzz watchers and tourists, pulling out to wait at the
hotel until night time?

It was hard to believe it of this pair of oldsters with their
grandmammy-grandpappy ways. But what happens to the
criminal types if they live to an advanced age? Don't they
grow old in crime? Age cannot wither nor custom stale their
felonious impulses.

Also what's to say they're as old as they look? It makes for
a great appearance of innocence and in body the old man at
least wasn't what anyone could call old.

"Erridge, my lad," I told myself, "you've been neatly
suckered. It's going to be morning before anyone comes up
here to look for you and by then they'll have been to the
gorge. They'll have pulled out whatever they have there and
they'll be off and gone."

Thinking some more, I began to persuade myself that it
couldn't work that well for them. There was Rachel and
Rachel was going to be the spoiler. She knew I'd gone up to
the room to pick up my light. How long would she expect
that to take?

A minute or two. Five minutes. Ten. She'd have to begin
wondering what was keeping me. She'd be coming up to
look for me or she'd be sending someone up to look. Pa
Haskin would volunteer to go up for her just in case I might
be changing my pants or something. He'd have that
covered. He'd have to, and anyhow that wouldn't be the
way Rachel would be thinking.

I go up for the light. I come down with it and I don't stop
to check in with her before going off to the gorge. I hadn't
said I'd check in with her before I went. She would think
that, once I'd pulled away from her, I was leaving it that
way just so she couldn't change her mind and insist on coming along. That was no good.

I looked for another straw to grab at and I came up with
Chief Joe Bowden. He had to come back sometime and he'd

come looking for me. I grabbed at it, but it was a lousy straw. I couldn't hold on to it. They didn't need me. Rachel could tell him everything we'd worked out and he could take off from there, leaving Erridge to turn up whenever Erridge got around to it. And that was if Bowden did turn up any time soon. Nobody knew where he'd gone or when he was likely to be back. What was to say he wouldn't be away and out of touch the whole night?

Even while I was giving up hope on Bowden, I was being bugged by a feeling of plain terror and I began asking myself what was triggering it. Something had passed through my mind and it was scaring the bewhatsit out of me before I could even pin it down and see what it was.

If Bowden turned up, he wouldn't need me. Rachel had the whole thing. She could tell him anything I could tell him.

SHE COULD TELL HIM.

I guess I'd been sweating right along and had been taking no notice of it, but switch from sweating a stream to sweating a glacier. You notice it.

What was he doing to Rachel?

It was no good lying there and thinking and it was no good thinking there was nothing else I could do. I could try. I had to try. I worked at channeling all my strength into my arms, trying to break my hands loose. If I could get them free, I could move. I could then untie my feet and get rid of the gag.

He had probably locked the door and gone off with the key, but that wouldn't make any important difference. I could crash the door down. It was a good, solid door but I had a good, solid shoulder. It would be good enough even though it was battered from knocking against all those rocks the night before.

I put everything I had into it and I couldn't manage even the slightest give. It was no good. I was just wasting my

strength. I had to try something else. I heaved and bounced
on the bed, trying to get it jumping up and down and banging against the floor. People would hear that. People would
come. If for nothing else, they'd come to give Erridge hell
for disturbing the peace of that quiet, respectable hotel.

It was a big bed and a heavy one. All my heaving and
flailing about was getting me nowhere. I was just bouncing
up and down on mattress and springs and not making
enough noise to disturb anyone. Nobody was hearing me.

I'd bounced myself to the edge of the bed and bounced
myself back to the middle. I had knocked the wind out of
myself and I had accomplished nothing. There had to be
something else I could try. I wasn't licked yet. I lay there for
a moment or two, thinking. Then I lay there for another moment or two, cursing myself for a dope. Rolling to the edge
of the bed, I'd caught myself short of rolling off and had
laboriously worked myself back to the middle.

How's that for stupidity? Down on the floor I could do
something. Thrashing around down there, I would be heard.
I could bang my heels against the floor. Here I'd been
sweating my guts out trying to bang the bed against the
floor when I didn't need it. I had put all that labor into
rolling myself back from where I should have wanted to be.

But it was all right. I'd made it to the edge before. I could
do it again and this time I would bounce myself off. I dug
my elbow in and started myself rolling. I had only just
flipped myself over on to my face when I heard the door
open. I froze.

If it was Haskin back again, let him think I was still out.
If it was Rachel or the chief, it wouldn't matter, but if it was
the enemy, he had me at every disadvantage. If I could take
him off guard, take him by surprise, catch him with a two-
legged kick and make it land some place that counted. If, if,
if.

I waited, saving myself for the one big effort. I knew I'd

get a chance for only one if he gave me even that. He wasn't hurrying. He shut the door quietly behind him. I wished I hadn't rolled over on my face. I would have liked to be able to see him, but then I thought it was maybe just as well. Face up, I would have had to keep my eyes closed till the moment when I was ready to stake everything on the one kick.

I could hear him walk across to the bed and come alongside it. He bent over me and checked the gag and the bindings on my hands and my feet. He was careful and he wasn't walking into anything. He had skirted the bed widely and didn't come in on me until he was up at the level of my head. Reaching from there he did his checking and there he was hopelessly out of range of a kick.

He had the whole thing figured. Move by move, he was ahead of me every step of the way. This was a careful man, sickeningly careful. He'd been to the gorge and he'd pulled out whatever it was he'd had there, and now they'd be taking off, but the careful man wasn't pulling out without first checking Erridge. Erridge had to be secured for long enough for Mom and Pa Haskin to be far far away before anyone would be alerted to go looking for them.

Did I say he was ahead of me every step of the way? I was thinking there was nothing more he could do that would surprise me and, brother, was I ever wrong? After completing his check, he took a solid grab on my arm and yanked me to the edge of the bed. Then, shifting his hold to my other arm, he rolled me, dumping me off the bed on to the floor.

It was where I'd wanted to be but I couldn't think he was doing me any favors. I couldn't figure what he was doing unless he was going to drag me off somewhere. Watching to stay away from my feet, he could drag me all over the place but only at the one level. If he was going to get me downstairs, he was going to have to sling me over his shoulder and carry me. I was wondering if he had worked out a way of doing that without giving me some chance to get my one big kick in.

I was trying to construct how it would have to go, trying to foresee the moment that, when it came, would be my moment. I would have to recognize it when it would be coming up. I had to be ready for it.

But he didn't drag me anywhere and he made no move toward slinging me over his shoulder. On the floor it was just more of the same. Grabbing me by the arm, he pushed me and he rolled me. There was a ruffled doohinkus that covered the bedspring and hung down to the floor. I felt that brush my face as he rolled me past it, when he pushed me under the bed. Once he had me under, he did some more tying. I couldn't figure just what. He wasn't adding to the stuff he had bound around me. He seemed to be tethering me to something by my arms and by my legs.

And that was it. I heard him go back to the door. I heard the key turn in the lock, the door open, the door shut, and the key again turn in the lock.

I lay there under the bed and I was laughing. It was all internal laughter that pushed against the gag and went nowhere, but while it lasted it was almost a good feeling. He was careful. He had everything planned. His planning was good and his execution was faultless, but now he had wigged out.

He rode along on his plan and, when he came up against the unforeseen, he improvised something to take care of it and set the plan to rolling once more. I had come blundering in on him the night before and he had dealt with me. I was getting in his way again this evening and he had dealt with me again, but then he'd learned that what he had done mightn't be good enough. People were beginning to wonder what had become of Erridge. Someone would get the idea of looking in the man's room. That wouldn't do, not if he was to be found trussed up on his bed before Mom and Pa had faded off beyond the horizon.

That called for another quick improvisation. Erridge is moved from on the bed to under the bed where he is effectively concealed by the doohinkus until morning when Day will come with her vacuum cleaner and, vacuuming under the bed, will suck old Matthew out of there.

Clever but on a quick improvisation a man can't think of everything. He hadn't thought that he was putting his prisoner just where Erridge wanted to be. So what were we waiting for? Let's bang that floor with all we've got. Let's knock the plaster off the ceiling down below.

I banged my heels against the floor and it wasn't as good as I'd hoped it would be. Under the bed I didn't have enough clearance to raise them up high enough to bring them down with as good a bang as I wanted. That could be remedied. He had rolled me under the bed, but I could roll myself out to the open floor and there I could do some man-sized banging.

I tried and, of course, I couldn't. He had tethered me to the four legs of the bed. He had made certain that I would remain hidden behind that ruffled whatsit. Again I was hauling and straining, trying to break loose. That wasn't any good, but in the process I discovered something that seemed great. I could hit that floor with more shattering bangs than I could have accomplished if I'd been free to jump up and down on it.

Heaving up against the underside of the bed, I found I could lift its heavy, massive frame off the floor. Collapsing quickly under it, I let it come down to hit the floor with a crash.

It wasn't easy. I couldn't get the whole of my back into it. With my hands tied behind my back, my arms got in the way. Each time I did it, the pressure on them made them feel as though I'd be wrenching them out of my shoulder sockets. Also I was mauling every bruise and scrape I had picked up the night before. I was giving myself one helluva battering but I couldn't care about that. I was shivering that hotel's timbers.

There was only one thing wrong with it. Nobody seemed to care. That made no sense. In even the most easygoing establishments they don't let guests carry on to that extent. There are limits and I was way out beyond them.

I kept at it till I didn't have another heave left in me. I had to stop and rest for a little while, if only until I could find some fresh strength. I lay still and tried to understand it.

As soon as I began thinking floor plan, it came to me. I'm not an engineer for nothing. I had the geometry of the building sitting in my head. I had just been forgetting to take it out and look at it. Nobody was being bothered by what I was doing because there was nobody under me to be bothered.

My room was over the second dining room, and the second dining room was not in daily use except in the high season when the summer visitors would have the hotel filled up. Out of season the second dining room was used only on weekends. It had been open the day before but that was because it had been Sunday. Now we were into Monday and back to just the one dining room. The second dining room was locked and empty. I had nothing to laugh at. He was still way ahead of me.

Just to lie there under that bed, trussed and tethered, would drive me crazy but all I could do was tell myself to keep hanging in there. I had no choice. I could wear myself out banging the bed against the floor but it would be an exercise in futility. I would do better saving my strength.

Saving it for what? When would I be given a chance to use it and meanwhile what had he done to Rachel?

I could lie there and spin myself fantasies and I fell into

doing just that. Sooner or later someone would come into the room. Sooner or later I would be turned loose. By that time, of course, he would be well away. Even while I was thinking it, it seemed a certainty that he was already well away and on his past record he would have been doing a great job of covering his tracks.

I told myself that it didn't matter how far he might go or how cleverly he might disguise his trail. If there was anything Erridge was going to do with the rest of his life, it would be tracking him down. What I imagined I might do to him when I did track him down I'm ashamed to tell you. There were all sorts of things and every last one of them as silly as it was sadistic.

There was one thing he hadn't foreseen and I comforted myself with that. He had tied me up under the bed with the idea that if anyone came to look for me, he would be confronted with what appeared to be an empty room and would go off to look for me elsewhere. He hadn't reckoned on the one thing I could do and that was bang the bed against the floor.

I lay there and I concentrated on somebody coming. I'd never gone for ESP or thought transference or even the efficacy of prayer, but I was down to that, to concentrating, to praying, to willing somebody to come into the room in search of me.

I concentrated and I prayed and I listened. My moment might not come, but if it did come, I had to be ready for it. At the first sound of anybody at the door, I was going to heave up and bang that bed against the floor. Nobody was going to open that door and not know that Erridge was there.

I lay there, saving myself for the moment, and the waiting seemed like a succession of eternities. There was a church clock that chimed the hours. After my first eternity I heard it strike but my mind hadn't been on it and it was already striking before I thought to count. I counted seven but I knew it was later than that. It had been just after seven when I'd come up for the lamp. Had there been one stroke before I began counting or two or more?

I waited through a second eternity before it struck again but then I was ready for it. I counted all of it and I came up with ten. Almost three hours had already gone and I had missed the eight o'clock chiming. I might have been knocked out then and not yet come to or I might have been so busy thrashing about or banging against the floor that I'd missed noticing it.

If the hour from nine to ten had seemed like a lifetime, the interval before I heard the clock strike again was more like Methuselah's lifetime. Then it came and again I counted it.

One. Two. Three. Four. Five. Six. Seven. Eight. Nine. Ten. Eleven.

No. It couldn't be. It mustn't be.

TWELVE.

What had become of eleven? My sweat went glacial again. Exhaustion had taken over and, without knowing it, I had dropped off. I had lain there under the bed and I had slept. How long I had no way of knowing, but this much I did know. While the clock was striking eleven, I had been asleep. For some of the time during that part of the evening when somebody might have come I had been hearing nothing. An obtrusive sound like the ringing of the hour hadn't penetrated my doze. Any small sound someone might have made coming to the room and looking in might have been even more easily missed.

I didn't know that anyone had come but I did know that I had missed out on the time when it had been most likely. Now after midnight it was hardly possible that anyone would still be coming. On any reasonable expectation I was stuck there until morning when Day would poke her vacuum cleaner under the bed.

The time when I'd had reason to be alert was gone. I had lost it. I could sleep. Now it would make no difference. I'd muffed it. So now I couldn't sleep even if I'd wanted to. I lay there hating myself, and self-reproach was keeping me wide awake.

I guess I worked at hating myself. Maybe it was a shield against giving the whole of my mind to the thought I couldn't push away. Where was Rachel? What had they done to her?

The stroke of one could have been a lot easier to miss than eleven had been, but I didn't miss it. It came and I heard it and I hated myself some more for hearing it. I worked at counting the remaining hours. Day started her work early. She'd already been at it when I came back to the hotel that morning, but then she had been cleaning up the downstairs and I didn't know whether she would be that early every morning. That had been Monday morning and she'd had the extra room to do, the dining room that had been used on the weekend. Tuesday morning there wouldn't be that room for her to do. Would that mean she'd start work later or that, spending less time downstairs, she would be coming up to the bedrooms earlier?

I didn't know. She'd done my room early that morning, but she had seen me. She had known I was up. This morning she wouldn't be seeing me. Wouldn't she be starting with the rooms she could get at? One-night-stand people would be up and on their way. She'd have their rooms to do. Erridge doesn't show. Early risers would be down to breakfast. She would have their rooms to do. You don't disturb Erridge. You let him sleep. You can do everything else before you come to his room. So when would that be? Late morning? Noon? Afternoon? Sometime people would have to begin wondering whether maybe there was something wrong with Erridge. They would be coming to check, but how many hours might it be till that happened?

Maybe it didn't have to wait that long. Day would be vacuuming the hall outside my door. She would be doing that early, possibly before she did up any of the rooms. That morning she had done my room before she did the hall but that had been only because she'd seen me and knew my room was available. If nobody would be up and out that early and she finished downstairs, certainly she would do the hall while waiting for the first room to be available.

Running the vacuum along the upstairs hall, bumping it against my door, that I would certainly hear. When I heard it, I'd bang the bed against the floor. She'd have to hear that. Or would she? She never heard anything over the noise of the vacuum. If you spoke to her, she had to switch it off or she couldn't hear you. Over the vacuum and through the door would she hear me however loudly I banged? I had to hope she would. The way things were running for me, I was ready to think she wouldn't.

Not through any hope of succeeding but only because I had to do something or go crazy, I went back to what I'd tried at the beginning. I strained against my bonds. I pushed. I pulled. I stretched. It was futile. I couldn't feel even the slightest give.

And then it happened. I had given up on expectation of anything but hearing the clock strike two and that was when they came, an indeterminate time after I'd heard the strike of one and before there was the strike of two.

I heard the key in the lock and I didn't wait to hear any more. I heaved up and lifted the bed. I collapsed under it and dropped it to the floor with a resounding bang. I kept doing it, deafening myself with my own noise. When I stopped he had already opened the door and was in the room.

He reached under the bed and patted me on the rump.

"Take it easy," he said. "Let me untie you."

I knew the voice. It was Andy. His hands were gentle and his voice was a soothing whisper. Getting me untied, he worked smoothly and efficiently. I wanted to tell him that he was beginning the process at the wrong end. I was exploding with unasked questions. I wanted the damn gag out of my mouth.

If he would only start with that, I could ask my questions. More than that, I could tell him to free my hands so I'd be able to work with him on the rest of the untying. But this was Andy, stupid old Andy. How bright could I expect him to be?

So he started with untethering me and pulling me out from under the bed. In my gratitude I made myself think that wasn't too stupid. Out on the open floor he'd have more room to work at the rest of it. In my impatience I hadn't recognized it, but maybe his way was the best, the quickest way to go about getting me completely freed.

But then he didn't go about it. He left the gag in my mouth. He left me tied hand and foot and, grabbing me by the shoulders, he started dragging me toward the door. That changed everything. I remembered the plan he had made for me. So the idiot was obsessed with it. Whether I liked it or not, Andy knew what was best for me. Andy was going to sneak me out of the country.

Not if I could help it. I started bucking and kicking, but he had expected that. He hadn't made the mistake of grabbing at my feet to drag me along. He had me by the shoulders where he was well out of kicking range. I fought him as best I could, doubling myself up and trying to butt him with my head.

All the time he was whispering to me.

"Oh, come on. Take it easy. Easy now. I'm getting you out of here. I know what you're up against and you don't. Come on, fella. Trust me."

The door opened and light from the hall fell into the room. Pa Haskin came in. Giving me a wide berth, he moved around beside Andy, well out of range of my kicking.

"Look, boy," he whispered. "We're your friends. We're doing this for you. Them tattooed crazies, they're all around the hotel and they're talking up a lynching. All that's holding them back so far is they don't know you're in here. They think you're off some place and they're watching for you to come back. Any time now they'll get tired of that and they'll come in here looking for you and then nobody can help you."

I wasn't buying it. I could see how the old bastard had suckered Andy into helping him by falling in with Andy's own crazy idea, but he wasn't suckering me. I had been there before. I had let him watch my back. I wasn't falling for that one again.

Andy gave up on me.

"You stay with him," he told the old man. "We'll never be able to get him out this way, not with him fighting us. We can't sneak him past anybody if he's going to be fighting us. I'll get something we can carry him in. You stay with him. I won't be a minute."

He took off and Haskin made another try at taming me with his talk.

"We're your friends," he said. "That Andy, he's got it all set up. We'll get you into this panel truck he's got parked out back and we'll drive you up through the woods. He's got a canoe in the truck. He'll get you over into Canada. It's only for a day, maybe two days. The Freeman girl knows the whole thing. She knows what we're doing. All you've got to do is stay up there and you can keep in touch by phone. You call Miss Freeman and give her a number up there where she can call you. As soon as this murder is cleared up and they've got the man who did it, she'll call and tell you and you'll come back. We don't get you out of here, you'll be dead before anything's cleared up."

Andy wasn't a minute. He came back with a big, covered, wicker basket. I'd seen it out in the hall many times. Day piled the laundry into it as she went from room to room changing the beds.

"Can't make him listen?" Andy asked.

"Just like he was from the first," Haskin answered. "He just won't see it that those thugs are dangerous."

Andy reached inside the windbreaker he was wearing and came up with a sock. It was a well-filled sock and I knew what it was filled with. Nobody needs a blackjack if he has a sock he can fill with sand. He came around back of me.

"I hate to do this," he said, "but it's the only way."

It was going to be the third time in twenty-four hours. How many times can a cat take it and not come out with his brains scrambled? There's never been the fight where the referee allowed a man to go down for more than one ten count, but this was no fight and to the list of things Erridge didn't have going for him you can add a referee.

For what happened next I can only reconstruct. I heard that whipping whoosh behind my ear, a sound to which I was getting all too much accustomed. I was blacked out for the rest of the removal from the hotel.

When I came out of it, I was in that big wicker hamper. The hamper was being lifted and tipped up and Erridge was being tumbled out of it. It was all quick. I was tipped out into the truck. The doors were slapped shut and I heard the bolts rammed home.

Within seconds the truck took off. It started with a jolt and I slid back to hit against the bolted doors. There was something else in that truck and it slid back to hit against me. It was soft and it was warm and it was mumbling softly.

I knew what it was. It was the last thing I wanted it to be, but I knew. This was what I'd been trying not to think. I could keep in touch with Rachel by telephone. She would tell me when it would be safe to come back. The lousy, lying killer. I was in touch with Rachel. Right there and right then I was in touch and it wasn't by telephone.

I tried to whisper her name but you can't whisper past a gag. You can only make those small, inarticulate sounds she was making. I wriggled around getting myself to where my hands could feel of her.

No, no, Charlie. Not what you're thinking. What do you take me for?

I felt of her face. I found a gag like the one I was wearing but that wasn't the whole explanation of her mumbling. There was more to it. Under the touch of my hands she didn't move. Except for the way the motion of the truck was jostling her, she was lying still.

I wriggled around some more, feeling first for her hands and then for her feet. Again it was the same. She was tied as I was, except that she had nothing at her knees, only the wrists behind her back and the ankles bound together. The only other difference was that she was tied up not with Atkinson's silk poplin but with rope. The rope took me back to the beginning. It stank of old fish.

I couldn't think about that, not just then. I couldn't think about anything but Rachel. She was warm. She was breathing. She was doing that mumbling behind her gag, but otherwise she was still. Still as death kept popping into my mind and I kept fighting the thought off. It was bad enough without any of that. The sand-filled sock behind the ear? Had they done that to the kid?

Then shouldn't she be coming out of it? I had. Could there be that much more bounce to me than there was in her? She was young. She was healthy. Why wouldn't she have the bounce? Had they hit her too hard? Had they used something more dangerous than the sand-filled sock? Was this concussion? Skull fracture?

I worked at not thinking any of that. It was no good. There was nothing I could do about it, not just then, if ever. I made myself work at finding the dimensions of this crazy thing that was happening to the two of us.

The old man had hung on in the bar for a while when we went in to supper. He had talked to Andy and Andy had told him of his scheme for getting me out of the country and how I was refusing to go along with it. It had been just what the old man needed. He would help Andy. They'd get me out whether I liked it or not. He would knock me out and tie me up in my room. I'd be all right there till Andy could shut up the bar and in the sleeping hotel they could get me out to the truck.

Haskin got me tied down and then they tried to sell Rachel on the idea but, of course she wouldn't go along with it and they were in trouble. She would blow the whistle on them. So they knocked her out and they were bringing her along and, by the time we could get back or even get to a phone Haskin would be off and gone.

He and Mom were probably already on their way with never the first worry about the problems Andy, the patsy, still had ahead of him. This part of it would be easy enough for him, driving to the woods and on up through the forest lands to the American side of the St. Croix. There he was going to have problems.

He was going to have to lift us out of the truck, launch the canoe, pick us up, dump us into the canoe without capsizing it, and paddle us across to the Canadian side where he would unload us and leave us. Leave us there all trussed up? He could hardly do that. Untie us, kiss us good-by, and paddle himself back alone to the American side? He had to know by now that I wouldn't be holding still for any of that. I was pretty sure Rachel wouldn't either if she ever came out of this nowhere they'd knocked her into.

Again with the sand-loaded sock? It was too much, too crazy.

Or was it crazy? I was breathing the fish stink off Rachel's ropes, that stink I had come to know too well Sunday night in the fish sack.

SUNDAY NIGHT!

Who's stupid now? Meathead Erridge, that's who.

X

Sunday down in Ogunquit he grabbed the bowl out of the hands of the man who couldn't see. The following Sunday Knees Coffin threw a party and Sam Ellsworth never got there. Sunday the whole town goes around with its tongue hanging out. No potent drink is sold anywhere. Hotel bar is closed on Sundays. Sunday is Andy's day off, and Rachel and I sat in Andy's bar and had him for an audience while we unraveled everything he thought he'd had safely tied up.

All that and the coffee-table book he kept shoving out of sight under the bar. Andy, suddenly gone studious, keeps hiding it away. *Early American Silver. Hallmarks of the Great Silversmiths.* That's the kind of stuff coffee-table books are made of. He took the bowl to Ogunquit and from the way the man down there felt of it, he caught on that he'd picked up something special this time. He stows it away and works at trying to learn how special it might be.

Maybe he asked some questions. Maybe he asked Sam Ellsworth. Maybe Ellsworth got suspicious of Andy's sudden and unprecedented interest in the finer things of life, particularly a finer thing that goes for a towering heap of bread. Ellsworth begins watching and snooping.

There had been things I should have caught and I'd missed them. When Andy reminded me that I had been in a fight and I had Ellsworth's button, he'd made a slip. Day had known about the button. Eddie Daisy Chain had known. They'd told Bowden. That much could have been all over the place, but not my abrasions and contusions. Nobody knew about those but Erridge, Bowden, and the man I'd met in the fog. He would know how he had pitched me down into the gorge and could guess that I'd come out of that beat up. There was no other way he could have known. Bowden had been nowhere near Andy after I'd told the chief and had shown him the scrapes and bruises. He had been with me and then he had taken off without a word to anyone else in the hotel. I knew that. I had seen him go.

It was true that I'd been around to the police station earlier and had left word that I wanted to report an assault and that the assault had been on me, but how could Andy have known that at a time when word of it hadn't even reached Bowden? Only one way: if he hadn't been the man in the fog, the man in the fog had confided in him. That latter was too hard to believe.

There had also been that stuff about what the post mortem was going to show up. They were going to find that Ellsworth had been dead before he'd gone into the river. How could Andy have known that unless he had been there, unless he was himself the killer? The man who had stowed the dead body away until the time was right for the tide to take it would need no post mortem to know.

I knew where I had gone wrong. I'd been so sure that Andy was stupid that I'd assumed he was too dumb to understand the difference between what he knew and what he had only as a wild guess. Because he was a dope about his bartending job, I'd tagged him for being a dope about everything. He was a lousy bartender because his heart was never in it. Get him in his own field, burglary, and he could be another man.

This way it works. This way it isn't crazy any more. It's just plain criminal and all the way up to and including murder. When a man's done one and he's about to have it pinned on him, he's not going to stop at two more if the two will get him unpinned.

He's not going to have any problems. Of course it will be the sand-loaded sock again. It won't matter if our brains are scrambled since we're never going to have any further mileage out of them anyhow. He'll knock us out, haul us out of the truck, drag us to the river, and hold our heads under water until we're drowned. Once we're as dead as a couple of surplus kittens, he unties us, dumps us in the river, and launches the canoe after us bottoms up.

That's it. We're a pair of killers skipping the country and not making it because a canoe is a tricky craft and we're too desperately in a hurry to be properly careful.

Haskin hadn't suckered Andy into helping him. That had been the other way around. Haskin had been easy. He was ready-made for it. As long as it was bad, there was nothing you could tell him about the Leather Vests that he wouldn't believe.

Andy fed him the lynch-mob fable and Pa fell for it hard. He fell for it so hard that it didn't bother him at all to take me from behind, knock me out, gag me, truss me up, and settle me comfortably on my bed. All that for him must have been like years ago when he took one of his kids out to the woodshed. If you had to hurt somebody for his own good, you didn't let any squeamish doubts stay your hand. You did your duty and you did a bang-up job of it. You're older and wiser and that's the only way to handle the young. You try to reason with them, but if they're stubborn and they persist in being unreasonable, you sock it to them for the good of their bodies and the good of their souls.

I was lying with my hands against Rachel's. Every jolt of the truck was rubbing my hands against hers. It gave me an idea. I could go with the truck. I didn't have to keep myself braced against the jolting. That's one of the things you do when you're trying to bring an unconscious person around. You chafe her hands.

We chafed like crazy the truck and I, but to no effect. My

hands kept hitting against the rope that bound her wrists and eventually I got the idea. I could feel the knot between my thumb and forefinger. Wriggling into a position that was as convenient for it as I could manage, I began working on the knot. It wasn't easy. It was slow work. The jostling of the truck jolted it out of my hand again and again. Bit by bit I loosened the knot and, after what seemed like the better half of forever, I got the damn thing undone. Her hands were free.

Her arms dropped to her sides. She didn't move them. Released from the rope, they just dropped. I wriggled around till I had myself in position to work on the other rope, the one around her ankles. That one was a little easier but only because now I knew the kind of knot he used. I wasn't wasting time and effort on tugging at the wrong part of it and pulling it tighter. Otherwise it was the same story, working at it, losing it when a heavy jolt jerked it out of my hand, finding it again, and working on it some more.

It took time, but eventually I had that one off and then I had to wriggle and squirm to get myself around to where I could do the rest of the job. It also involved a lot of pushing against her, shoving her over to make myself squirming room. The space was narrow. There was something big and hard with us in that truck and it wasn't until I'd done a lot of squeezing past it that I dug what it was. I should have known. It had to be there. It was the canoe.

I finally got myself squeezed past it and I was in position for working on the third knot, the one at the back of her head. That wasn't rope. It was a scarf or a handkerchief or something of that sort and it wasn't knotted as tightly as the ropes had been. It didn't have to be. All it was doing was holding the gag in place. Once I got my hand on that one, I had it undone in jig time.

Feeling it come loose, I had a momentary thrill of triumph, but it didn't last past the moment. I wanted her to reach up and pull the gag out of her mouth. I wanted her at least to move her lips, to make some unconscious effort to spit the thing out. She didn't move.

I had to wriggle around some more so that I could get my hand to her lips. I caught hold of the wad of stuff she had rammed in her mouth and I yanked it out. I could move my fingers but I couldn't move my hands, not enough to make it. I had to move them the only way I could by carrying them along with my whole body. I got a firm hold on the gag between my thumb and forefinger and, hanging on to it, I rolled away from her. That's how I yanked the gag out.

Don't ask me to explain what I did next. All I know is I wanted to do it and I thought I could. It took another wriggling and squirming squeeze back through some of that narrow space between her body and the canoe. I didn't have to go all the way back to where I'd been working on her ankles but did have to make it half the way, to where I'd be wedged in tightest.

I beat myself up doing it, putting a fresh abrasion on my every contusion and a fresh contusion on my every abrasion as I banged and scraped against the bed of the truck and the canoe. When her hair brushed my cheek, I knew I was coming close. I rolled a bit, bracing myself against the truck's jolting, fighting to hold my position. I brought my mouth up against hers and I tried to kiss her.

Of course, it wasn't any good. How could it be with my kisser under wraps? Don't ask me how I could ever have expected anything of it when it couldn't be anything but pushing my gag and the thing that was tying it in against her lips?

Maybe if I could have made it a real kiss, I could have done some magic. As it was, nothing came back at me. She was motionless, inert.

I pulled away from it and every one of my fresh bruises and scrapes had come alive. I welcomed them. They were talking to me and what they were saying brought me a surge of fresh hope. I'd rubbed myself raw against the canoe when what I should have been rubbing against it was the silk that held my wrists.

I didn't have to wriggle around to get into position for it. I was there. All I had to do was saw away. That silk poplin is strong stuff; I could never have ripped it or made it split, but there's nothing that won't abrade.

I worked at it and again it was the way it had been when I'd been chafing Rachel's hands. The jolting of the truck was in there helping me, but now I was getting a bigger assist. The jolts were heavier and more frequent than they had been. I could dig that. We'd come off the pavement and we were now on the dirt road through the woods. It was a rough ride and I loved its every bump.

I rubbed and I pulled. It took a long time, but I knew where we were going. It's a long ride up through those woods before you hit the St. Croix. I didn't let myself think about whether it was going to be long enough. It had to be.

If you ever want evidence that sex is more in the head than in any of the expected areas, you can call Erridge for a witness. There I was wedged in tight between Rachel and the canoe and I was working on freeing my hands. I was putting everything I had into rubbing the silk against the canoe and in the process I was bumping against that beautiful body, pressing her tight against all of me, rubbing against her with all of me.

Maybe you won't believe me and all I can do is give you my word for it but it was just as though it wasn't happening. I felt nothing. Nothing stirred in me. Looking back on it now, just remembering where I was and where she was and what I was doing, I work up a storm of desire but then I felt nothing but the weakening of the silk.

I can remember the moment when, straining my wrists apart, I felt the first slight give. I was getting there, just a little more and I'd have it. Then it wasn't just a little more. I went on and on, ignoring the growing ache in my arms and shoulders. Have you ever felt your arms go numb? They're hurting like they've maybe never hurt before but they're going numb and the numbness, which ought to be dulling the pain, is doing nothing. If anything, it's making the pain worse.

Bit by bit, though, I felt a little more give and a little more. Then suddenly the silk snapped and my hands were free. What I wanted most then was to get rid of the gag. I'd been living with it far too long a time. I was sick with the taste of it. For all that I was pouring spit to the place where I was choking on it, my mouth felt like a bag of dust. The saliva was there but it wasn't wetting anything but the damn gag.

I made myself remember first things first. If I had a chance to go into action I could do it with the gag in my mouth. With my legs still tied I'd never have a chance.

The rest of it was quick and easy. With my hands free, I could get to my pocket knife. Cutting myself free at knees and ankles was only a moment's work. After that I allowed myself the luxury of ridding myself of the gag. I thought of keeping the knife in my hand but decided the blade was too short for doing anything quick and decisive. I shut it and slipped it back into my pocket.

Rachel was mumbling again but now it wasn't inarticulate. I listened hard, trying to make some sense of it, but she was just saying the one word over and over and it wasn't even a real word.

"Alexandy," she muttered. "Alexandy."

I grabbed for her and I shook her. I felt for her face. I located her cheeks. I slapped her hard.

"Alexandy," she said.

Now she was speaking it. It wasn't a mumble any more. We hit a big bump and my belly hit hard against the canoe.

It hit with a loud clunk and that's never the sound a belly makes when it hits anything. The belly sound is more like an ooof. I felt it as well, something banging hard into my gut.

I put my hand down to feel for what it was and I couldn't believe it. It was that lamp of mine, the one I'd been going to pick up when Pa Haskin sapped me. I wasn't asking how it got there. It could have been another like mine but I didn't believe it. It was hooked over the gunwale of the canoe. When I'd hit against it, it had banged against the side of the canoe. It had to be that Andy had picked it up and brought it along. Maybe he'd been thinking it would look better if my body was found with the lamp on me. People would think I'd needed it for the woods and for the river crossing in the dark. Maybe he'd figured on it coming in handy as a light to murder us by. I was guessing that he'd picked it up when he came up to the room to check me, roll me under the bed, and tether me there.

I felt for the switch and found it but, before I flipped it, I snatched my hand away. There were things I had to know about that truck before I could think of lighting it up. Some of them have a window between the cab and the body of the truck. Some aren't partitioned at all. Only the back of the driver's seat separates the front from the body of the truck.

The last thing I wanted to do was give him any forewarning. If I was ever going to get the jump on him, it was only going to be if he came after me in the expectation that he was going to find me all trussed up and handleable, not up on my feet and ready to swing. There would be a moment when I might have the advantage of him. I couldn't throw it away.

The truck would stop. He'd have to come down out of the cab and come around to open the rear doors. I would know when he was coming and I would have all the time I would need for getting ready for him. He would open the doors.

With him down on the ground and me up in the truck I'd have the elevation on him. Jump him from above? Kick him in the face?

It was going to depend on just how he would be standing when he opened the doors. I was going to have to see and, when I saw, my reflexes would take over. I was telling myself that I could trust my reflexes. In any event I would have no choice. There would be nothing else going for me.

Moving in the dark, I felt my way back through the truck. I was down on all fours just in case there was no partition. When I came to it, it was all right. I wasn't up against a seat back. There was a partition. As long as I had my mind all wrapped up with giving myself some light, what I was finding seemed encouraging; but some part of my mind broke loose and shot me all through with disappointment.

If there had been no partition, I wouldn't have had to wait for him to come to me. I could have jumped him while he drove, grabbed him by the throat perhaps or conked him on the head with the lamp. I sure owed him that much, at least one good, crunching conk on the head.

Tight up against the partition, I rose up slowly and carefully. I still didn't know whether or not there would be a window and if there was a window whether it would be shut or open. I had started out hoping for no window, but now I reversed. I wanted one and I wanted it to be open. The thought of conking him on the head was too enticing.

You know how it goes. You can't have everything. There was no window, just the unbroken, blind partition all the way up to the roof of the truck. I had been going along with a pretty good opinion of my thinking and now I had a moment of doubt. All that careful checking for a window when I should have known there couldn't be one there. If there had been a window, there would have been some light coming through it.

I explored the partition with my finger tips, feeling for

slits or cracks, feeling along where it joined the roof of the truck and where it joined the sides, making certain that there would be no fissure that could leak light.

It was snug and solid all the way around. I switched on the light. Most of what it showed me was what I already knew by feel. There was the canoe. There were two paddles. There was a heap of mangled silk that had once been some of my favorite ties and they were where I dropped them when I got them off me. There were a couple of wet handkerchiefs, Rachel's gag and mine.

There was Rachel. She was lying where I'd left her, but she moved. Some of the movement was not her own. It was the jolting of the truck that moved her, but there was more of it and that was her own. It was a little snuggling wriggle, a stab toward finding a more comfortable position in sleep.

For the moment I had to tear my eyes away from Rachel to take in the rest of it. There were the ropes with which she had been tied. They were like my ties, lying where I'd dropped them. At the back of the truck, however, right at my feet, where I was standing backed against the partition, there was more rope, another set like the ones that had been used for binding and gagging Rachel, and alongside them was another handkerchief, but this one was dry. Unlike the other two, it wasn't spit-soaked from having been stuffed into anyone's mouth.

I tried to understand that. I felt I couldn't disregard it. I couldn't allow myself to disregard anything. The more I knew about what I was going up against, the better the chance that my reflexes would zero in on the right target.

All I could make of it was that the extra ropes and the extra handkerchief, these supplies that hadn't been used, must indicate a change of plan. He had prepared two sets, one for Rachel and one for me; but then he'd had the chance to do it an easier way. He had suckered Pa Haskin into taking care of me. Since the old man had done it up in my hotel room, he hadn't had Andy's prepared supplies in hand and he'd made do with what was convenient—my ties, my handkerchief.

It seemed a reasonable answer and, furthermore, it was the only one I could come up with. It left me free to go back to where my thinking wanted to be—to Rachel. She lay there sleeping like a baby and it looked like normal sleep, deep sleep but only that, nothing like coma. If I worked at it, I was sure I could rouse her, but I asked myself if I wanted to work at it.

I did want to. I wanted it and passionately, but I was having some other thoughts. If she was awake and on the move when Andy came to open the doors, could I be sure that she wouldn't get in the way of what I had to do? I could move her deep into the truck, settle her there as comfortably as I could manage, and let her sleep. That way I'd have nobody to worry about. I could move in on Andy with nothing to distract me from what I had to do, taking him before he could know what hit him.

I moved toward her, all set to do it that way, but even before I'd reached her, I knew it was wrong. I couldn't do it.

"Erridge," I told myself, "you're a male chauvinist pig."

Who was I to take it all on myself, dispose of her life for her, give her no choice but to let everything hang on my chance of success? Andy opens the door. I jump him. I'm even a little bit unlucky. My first charge doesn't dispose of him and I'm not able to take him. He takes me. After all, the Erridge skull has soaked up three sand-bagging massages and Andy hasn't had even one.

I feel ready and able. I even feel lucky, but that's no guarantee that I will be. Suppose it goes wrong and he does take me. She falls into his hands asleep and she's never had a chance to do the first thing for herself. I'd be delivering her to him on a silver platter and that he doesn't rate. He already has a silver bowl.

If I miss and I don't take him, if in the end he does take me, there is this much I will be able to do. I am going to make damn certain that I'll do at least this much. I'll keep him tied up tangling with me long enough for Rachel to get away. Of course, I'll be going for the whole thing, but I can't kid myself that it'll be any lead-pipe cinch. He had taken Sam Ellsworth and I'd been told that Ellsworth had been a lot of man. This much, though, I was guaranteeing myself. I would at least hold him off long enough to let Rachel grab at her chance to live.

But first I had to wake her and I had to make her understand what was going on. I had to get her drilled in what she was going to have to do. It was going to be touch and go, no time for mistakes and no time for hesitations, but all that was needed was that she should be on her feet and knowing exactly what her job was.

I doused the light. For what I had to do I didn't need it. I went to her and shook her. Again she spoke in her sleep and again it was the same old garble.

"Alexandy."

I pulled her to her feet and holding her tight against me to steady her against the bumping and lurching of the truck I kept her upright and I walked her. I dragged her. I propelled her. I kept her on her feet and I kept her moving. There wasn't much room for it. It was back and forth, back and forth in the narrow confines of that little truck. Those confines, you've got to remember, were made even narrower by the canoe we had sharing the space with us.

It happened slowly. It was a gradual thing. In its beginnings it was almost imperceptible, but it was happening. Little by little I felt myself bearing less of her weight. Her knees were still rubbery. If I'd let go of her, she would have sagged down to the floor, but the limpness was going out of the rest of her. She was beginning to hold herself erect. She was doing it with much of my help, but bit by bit she was putting something of herself into it.

Then she spoke.

"Andy," she said. "What's wrong with me, Andy?"

I held her with one hand, freeing the other to switch on the light.

"Not Andy," I said. "Matt. Matt Erridge. Remember?"

She looked at me and she blinked.

"Matt," she said. "You went off. You just went without stopping by even for a moment. You just went and you were gone for the longest time."

"I know," I told her. "I wanted to come back, but I couldn't. What happened to you?"

"I don't know."

"I left you in the bar with Andy. Try to remember. You were in the bar with Andy waiting for Joe Bowden to turn up and waiting for me to come back. What happened then?"

"You were gone the longest time and I began worrying. I got the shakes. Somebody said I needed a drink. Somebody."

"Who? Remember who."

"Andy. Yes, Andy. He said I needed a drink and he fixed me an Alexander. He said he'd watched you make them and he knew how. He didn't really. I mean he didn't really know how."

"It didn't taste right?"

A crazy question. What kind of a praise-seeking half-wit bothers with a question like that at such a time?

"Not like yours. It wasn't much good. It had a peculiar taste, but what could I expect? You hadn't made it. Andy did, and you know Andy. He's no quick study."

"Listen, baby," I said, "and listen hard. Stupid Andy isn't stupid about everything. Some things he's too smart about, things like mixing a Mickey. You know what a Mickey is?"

"Mickey Finn?"

"That's right, a doped-up drink. A drink that will put you right out and keep you out for hours. His Alexander didn't taste like mine because mine didn't have the extra ingredient. Mine weren't Mickey Finns."

"Andy?"

"Andy who doesn't work Sundays. Andy who went down to Ogunquit on a Sunday. Andy who was too stupid to know what he'd ripped off but who learned down in Ogunquit that he'd ripped off something that might be special. Andy who's been keeping a big book under the bar and who's been very careful that nobody should see what book it is because he's studying that book trying to learn what it is he's got stowed away somewhere in the gorge."

"You found it?"

"No. He knocked me out before I could go and look. He knocked me out and left me tied up in my room. That's why I couldn't come back."

It wasn't exactly accurate but right then there was no need for explaining how he'd suckered Pa Haskin into helping him. It would only complicate things and slow us up. There was too much I had to tell her and not all the time in the world for doing it. The details I could give her later.

"Where are we now, Matt?"

"He has us locked up in a truck and he's driving us through the woods up to the St. Croix. He had us both tied, hand and foot and gagged. When you passed out he must have brought you out to the truck."

"I remember," she said. "I began feeling woozy. He said I needed air. He walked me outside. I remember that, but it's all I remember."

"Then he got you outside before you passed out," I told her. "He tied you and gagged you and left you in here trussed up and unconscious. After he closed the bar, he dragged me down from upstairs and dumped me in here with you. I got myself loose and untied you. He won't be expecting that."

"His crazy idea that you would run for Canada before Joe Bowden arrests you?"

"We both run for Canada because you know as much as I do and he has to get rid of the both of us. When we get up to the river, he's going to come and take us out of here, drag us to the river bank, drown us, untie and ungag us, push us into the river, and push the canoe in after us bottom up."

She took a long breath.

"We'll be the killers," she said. "It'll be that we were running away and we didn't make it across the river. We drowned."

"Except that it won't be that way. When he put us in here, we were a pair of securely tied packages. He's going to come and open the door, expecting to find us that way, securely tied packages he can handle without any trouble. He won't know that we're loose and that'll give me the jump on him."

"It'll give us the jump on him," Rachel said. "We'll be two against one."

"That we will," I said, "and if we both of us do exactly what we have to do, we'll have Andy where we want him and we'll be okay."

"What do I do?" she asked. "Tell me."

"There's no chance of his taking us by surprise this time," I began. "We'll know when he's coming. He has to stop the truck, come down out of the cab, and come around to open the doors. We'll be ready for him."

"That we will," she said.

She balled up her fists. I took the two of them in one of my hands.

"You'll be right behind me," I said. "Before he even has his hands off the doors, I'll jump him. The minute I jump, you must jump, too."

"Don't worry about me. I'll do my part. We'll jump him together."

"No," I said. "We'll only get in each other's way. He'll be my job. You'll have yours."

She jerked her hands out of mine.

"The weak, little woman will stand back and organize a cheering section," she growled. "I'll jump up and down. I'll yell, 'Rah, Erridge, rah, rah, rah.' Then I'll turn a cartwheel. Why didn't you think to bring a baton for me to twirl?"

I grinned at her.

"That would be nice, great ego-building for me," I said, "but there won't be time for it. You'll jump past me, run around to the front of the truck, climb up into the cab, and take off."

"Leaving you to fight him alone? Not on your life."

"You'll drive off and get help. When you come back with the troops, you'll find me waiting for you and I'll have Andy all tied up and waiting with me. I probably won't gag him. It might be interesting to hear what he has to say, but that will depend on how long you're gone. If I get bored with what he's saying, I can always gag him then."

"Suppose he has a knife or a gun. Suppose he kills you?"

"We'll be at close quarters," I said. "If I have a man at close quarters, I know how to take a gun away from him and I know how to take a knife away from him. Also you're forgetting that I'll have the jump on him. I'll be taking him by surprise."

"I don't know. It could go wrong. He might kill you."

I had to concede it. Anything else would have me sounding like a blowhard. That's never a persuasive sound. I tried to sound practical and realistic.

"He might. I'll be surprised if he does. The odds say I will take him, but if he does kill me, it won't make me any less dead if he gets to kill you as well. If we give him the chance, he's going to kill us both. He's committed to it. There's nothing else he can do now."

"You stand and fight him," she moaned, "and I run like a coward."

"I stand and fight him," I told her, "and you run to bring me the help I'll need. You'll run because you're no coward. You're not a hysteric who goes paralyzed in an emergency. You've got guts. You're not afraid to drive through the woods alone at night."

"Can't we think of another way? There must be another way."

"You stand and take him while I go for help?" I said. "Have you had any experience with taking a knife away from a man or a gun? Just convince me that you're qualified and we'll do it your way."

"Damn you," she said. "You know I'm not."

"Look, baby," I told her. "It's no fault of yours. You didn't ask to be brought up in a world that's run by male chauvinist pigs who trained men in these nasty skills and never gave women a shot at them. I could teach you how it's done, but it takes time and practice and time is what we haven't got."

"I'll hate myself," she said.

"But I'll love you."

I thought it was a good line but it did nothing toward selling her. I tried another tack.

"There's another factor," I said. "You were fed the Mickey and I wasn't. I can rely on my reflexes. I haven't had anything to slow me up. You can't rely on yours. It'll wear off. It's mostly worn off already. You're doing fine, but you're not completely yourself yet. You can't expect to be. So you'll do the part of the job you can do. You're in good enough shape to drive."

She sighed.

"I do feel a little numb and more than a little thick in the head," she admitted.

"It's not you," I assured her. "It's the Mickey. In time it'll pass off. You'll be as good as new. Meanwhile you're going to be more than good enough."

We talked some more. We sat on the canoe and rested for what was ahead of us. I filled her in on details, the Pa Haskin part of it, how Andy had worked on him with that story about the Leather Vests working up to a lynching. Hearing about Pa worried her.

"That could change everything, Matt," she said. "What if he has Mr. Haskin along with him? What will we do then?"

"Not possible. He has to kill us and he can't do that with Haskin to witness it."

I repeated to her what Pa had said to me, how I was to keep in touch from Canada by phoning her.

"He can't have the old man along," I said. "Haskin doesn't know you're here. If he ever saw you, he'd know Andy had been lying to him. Andy used the old man for taking care of me while he himself was busy taking care of you. That's all he needed Haskin for. He couldn't bring him along up here."

"It's wonderful how you've figured the whole thing out," she said.

"I had it knocked into my head," I told her.

So then she kissed me.

If you're adding up the score I had against Andy, don't forget to count this in. At just that ill-chosen moment he slowed the truck and brought it to a stop. It was battle stations and no time for the better things in life.

I took up position just inside the doors. She was directly behind me. We heard the bolts rattle as they were pulled back. The doors swung open and the opening was silvery with moonlight.

I aimed my kick. It was going to be easy. Taking it full in the face, no man could stand up under it. Teeth go, nose breaks, eyes go blinded with blood and pain, and long before he can begin to know what hit him, the knockout blow has come in behind it.

I aimed it. I swung it. It was a clean miss. He ducked down under it and there was no explaining that. It hadn't been that he'd seen it coming. I hadn't telegraphed it. It was the instantaneous thing. It would have landed before he could possibly have seen it.

I had been counting on my reflexes and what I got instead was momentum. You kick and you put your whole body weight behind the kick. When your foot meets its target, you come into equilibrium and you stay on your feet. My foot met nothing. So the kick described a much longer arc than I was prepared for and the rest of my body followed through. The momentum carried me off the tail of the truck and bounced me down hard on my ass, but I didn't hit the ground.

I came down on Andy. While it was happening I had no way of knowing who was where or what was going on but it reconstructed easily enough afterward. He was crouched down bent over something on the ground and I landed on him with all my weight plus the propulsion of my aborted kick. I hit him on the back about the level of his shoulders and his neck. He flattened under me, but he immediately unflattened to squirm around and try for a grip on me.

I wasn't giving him the time for that. I slid down his back just far enough to get my hand in and I chopped him. He went limp under me. I rolled off him and I was fumbling for my belt as I rolled. I was going to use it to tie up his hands. I could take his own belt off him and it would do for securing his ankles.

Then Rachel spoke to me.

"Matt," she said. "Look, Matt, the poor old man."

I looked and it was all laid out before me. Pa Haskin was on the ground. He was out cold and Rachel was kneeling beside him doing the wrist-chafing bit. I looked down at Andy's hand. He still had the sand-loaded sock gripped in it.

I had been right and I had been wrong. He couldn't let Pa Haskin see Rachel. In that I was right, but he couldn't leave Haskin behind. I had missed out on digging that. Come morning, Haskin would have learned that there had never been any lynching threat and, when our bodies were found, Rachel's and mine, Haskin would have had too much of a tale to tell.

One murder, two, three. Might as well make it four and be safe. He took Pa Haskin with him. For company? For help with getting us across to Canada? He let the old man pull the bolts on the truck doors. By then Pa would have been eager to have me out of the truck and untied and ungagged. He hadn't been happy about what he'd had to do to me. Can't you just hear him saying that it hurt him more than it did me?

So Pa pulled the bolts and Andy, standing behind him, brought him down with the loaded sock. That was why Andy's head hadn't been where it should have been when I kicked out at it. He hadn't seen anything. He'd stooped down to make sure the old man was effectively knocked out and would stay that way till he could haul us out of the truck and fish out the extra ropes and the extra gag he'd brought along for Pa.

I was taking no chances. I fastened him up good with my belt and his, and only then I moved over to help Rachel with the old man. His pulse and his breathing were all right. He would be coming out of it in a few minutes. Rachel left me with him for a moment while she went the few steps to the river bank to soak her handkerchief in the ice water that runs in those rivers up there. Coming back with the dripping handkerchief, she pressed it against the old man's forehead. He began stirring.

"I ought to slug you," I told Rachel.

"I know, Matt, but I saw the poor old man and everything just went out of my head."

"It's a good lie," I said. "You never meant to take off even though we'd agreed."

She smiled.

"You'll never know," she said. "Will you now?"

"I suppose if I tell you to do something, I can't expect you to do it," I said.

"It depends on what it is."

"Get me the ropes out of the truck, the ones Andy never got to use."

She looked stricken.

"You're going to tie Mr. Haskin up?" she gasped.

"No. Just make things doubly sure on Andy."

She brought me the ropes and I used them around the lug's elbows and knees. I wasn't contributing to his comfort but I was taking no chances with him. Remembering the job he'd done on Rachel, furthermore, I pulled the ropes tighter.

Between Rachel's urgings and her icy water Pa Haskin came to and sat up. It took him a moment or two to get himself unscrambled. What confused him most was Rachel's being there though he also had to adjust to me being on the loose and Andy trussed up, but he wasn't fighting it. At long last he knew the score. He had been opening the doors to get me out of the truck and Andy had come up behind him and sapped him. Could he ask for anything more to make the whole thing come clear?

While we were loading Andy into the truck, we filled the old man in on what he didn't know and he filled us in on what we didn't know. He gave us nothing new. That was all as I guessed it had to be, Andy was back among the conscious but he was saying nothing. I think he preferred to listen to us. He was learning just how deep he was sunk.

I thought we'd be riding back out of the woods with the

three of us in the cab of the truck. That would have meant Rachel between Haskin and me and everything nice and tight and close. Pa had other ideas. He insisted on riding back with Andy. After all he'd done me up so well and I had worked my way out of it. He, for one, saw no reason for taking any chances on Andy doing as well.

"I'll ride in back where I can keep an eye on the devil," he said. "If he even tries to get his hands free, it'll be my chance to kick his brains out."

It wasn't all that tight and close riding back, but it was just the two of us and the woods and the moon.

I've had it worse, Charlie. I've had it a lot worse.